CRACKER!
THE BEST DOG IN VIETNAM

CRACKER!
THE BEST DOG IN VIETNAM

CYNTHIA KADOHATA

Aladdin Paperbacks
NEW YORK   LONDON   TORONTO   SYDNEY

ALADDIN PAPERBACKS
An imprint of Simon & Schuster Children's Publishing Division
1230 Avenue of the Americas, New York, NY 10020
Text copyright © 2007 by Cynthhia Kadohata
All rights reserved, including the right of reproduction in whole or in part in any form.
ALADDIN PAPERBACKS and related logo are
registered trademarks of Simon & Schuster, Inc.
Also available in an Atheneum Books for Young Readers hardcover edition.
This book is only available in the school book club and school book fair market.
Designed by Ann Zeak
The text of this book was set in Garamond BE.
Manufactured in the United States of America
First Aladdin Paperbacks edition August 2008
2 4 6 8 10 9 7 5 3 1
The Library of Congress has cataloged the hardcover edition as follows:
Kadohata, Cynthia.
Cracker!: the best dog in Vietnam / Cynthia Kadohata.—1ˢᵗ ed.
p. cm.
Summary: A young soldier in Vietnam bonds with his bomb-sniffing dog.
[1. German shepherd dog—War use—Juvenile fiction. 2. Dogs—War use—Fiction.
3. Vietnam War, 1961–1975—Fiction. 4. Human-animal relationships—Fiction.] I. Title.
PZ10.3.K1005Cr 2007
[Fic]—dc22   2006022022
ISBN-13: 978-1-4169-0637-7 (hc.)
ISBN-10: 1-4169-0637-1 (hc.)
ISBN-13: 978-1-4169-7522-9 (Scholastic ed.)
ISBN-10: 1-4169-7522-5 (Scholastic ed.)

To my editor, enforcer, and great friend, Caitlyn Dlouhy,
and to the brave dogs and men who served together in Vietnam.

One

GRRRR! FOR I AM THE ALL-POWERFUL CRACKER! Cracker spotted a bird carcass lying in the alley. She picked it up between the tips of her front teeth and flipped it into the air, growling as it sailed above her. When it plopped down, she pushed at it with a paw. She growled more, then leaned the side of her head on the asphalt, staring right into its face. It might have been dead for a week, but who cared? She would kill it again. That's how powerful she was. She hopped to her feet to attack it—and spotted a mouse! Alive! This was for real! She took off.

Somewhere in the background she heard a voice calling, "Cracker! Cra-a-a-acker! Cracker!"

The mouse had a head start, but she would catch him. She bounded forward and leapt through the air just as the mouse slipped through a chain-link fence.

She reared up and pawed higher on the fence, pushing wildly at the metal to search for weakness. The mouse didn't move. Just sat in the dirt. Cracker whined. She even licked the fence in the place where the mouse had slipped through. She thought she could just taste his fur . . . *mmmm.*

She reached her paw into a loose area of chain near the ground, but the mouse sat just out of reach. It was as if he were taunting her now. She. Was. Going. To. Kill. That. Mouse. She stared at him as hard as she could. There was nothing in the world except for her and that mouse.

"It's just a mouse," Willie said, out of breath from chasing her. "It's dead. D-E-A-D. Dead."

Cracker started. She had almost forgotten about Willie. But he didn't sound angry. Her ears perked. She could hear Willie's mother calling. Willie picked up a stick and poked at the mouse, sending it scampering. *Huh?* Cracker looked at Willie sorrowfully: Why had he made the mouse go away?

"Oh, stop it," said Willie. Then he said, "Good girl," rubbing Cracker's head. All thoughts of the mouse drained quickly from Cracker. She wagged her tail. *Good girl!* She didn't even glance at the bird as she and Willie trotted toward home. Who cared about a dead bird?

Willie petted her head again. "Shake!" Willie said, and she fell over . . . no, that was "play dead." She leapt up in the air and ran in a circle around him. He laughed, and they continued down the alley.

Willie felt invincible as he walked with Cracker. His mother was used to a better neighborhood and didn't like them walking through the alley in the evenings, but Cracker's muscles were stronger than any man's, and Willie always felt safe with her. Willie's father had worked as foreman of a taffy apple factory, but when he was laid off, they'd had to move to an apartment while he worked a lower-paying job. And the apartment didn't allow dogs. The landlord had given Willie's family one month to get rid of Cracker. That was twenty-five days ago. Willie felt a sharp pain in his stomach at the thought.

Cracker felt Willie's unhappiness and whined. When they stopped in front of their apartment building, Willie suddenly fell to the ground in front of her and hugged her so hard, it actually kind of bothered her neck. What was going on? "You're the best dog in the world," Willie said. "Good girl!" Willie stood up again and looked sadly at Cracker. Anxiety filled her. She jumped up and placed her paws on Willie's shoulders, almost knocking him over. Willie cracked a smile, and Cracker felt a little better.

At the top of the stairs she scratched at the door to his third-floor apartment. She could never open that door. Willie had to use his "key." Every day he did the same thing: held up the key and said to her as if she were slow-witted, "Key. Need key." At the other place they'd lived, the door had pushed open when she grabbed her paws just right around the knob.

Willie opened the door and immediately headed for the bathroom. "Mom, I'm gonna take my bath!" He didn't want his parents to see him crying. They already felt bad enough. But he hesitated just inside the bathroom as he thought maybe he *did* want them to see him crying. Maybe then he would be able to keep Cracker. But he knew that wasn't true. He'd already cried a lot, and nothing had changed. Crying wouldn't get his father's job back. He closed the door.

"All right!" he could hear his mother call out. She and his dad were watching TV.

He took off his Cubs jacket. As far as Willie was concerned, the Cubs were going to win this year's Eastern Division, and Willie thought about them almost as much as he thought about Cracker. Some people thought the stupid Mets or Pirates would win the division. Willie wasn't allowed to use the word "stupid" out loud, but he liked to think the word to himself whenever he felt annoyed.

He'd heard his father use the word just once, during an argument with his mother about the Vietnam War. His parents, uncle, and aunt were all playing bridge, and then all of a sudden they were yelling about the war. There were several hundred thousand American troops in Vietnam, and every day the news reported protests against the war. Ever since Willie's favorite cousin, Derrick, had been drafted, Willie wrote all his school current events reports about Vietnam. Willie's father supported the war, and his mother didn't. And then with the job layoff and the move, well, things weren't going that well for Willie.

Except for the fact that Cracker was a girl and Willie was a boy, Cracker and Willie were—as his mother liked to say—peas in a pod: They both weighed 110 pounds, and they were almost the same age, Willie eleven in human years and Cracker one year and four months, which Willie had decided was actually eleven in dog years. They both had sandy brown hair in the exact same shade. And Mom also pointed out that Cracker and Willie thought alike. For instance, they probably agreed on two of the biggest problems in their lives: that they lived in a small apartment without a yard and that Willie went away for several hours a day. But once Willie came home from school, life was pretty much perfection, even without a yard. They went out to play with the neighborhood kids until dark, came inside for dinner, went outside for a walk, and then slept on their twin bed together.

And now Cracker was about to make Willie's life miserable. But he just smiled at her. He'd tried to tell her, but she hadn't understood.

Cracker felt life was bliss too, though it wasn't quite perfection, and for precisely the reasons that Willie's mom thought. Furthermore, Cracker considered Willie a bed hog, but if Cracker held her ground, Willie behaved himself and squeezed up against the wall while she stretched out across the bed, with maybe just a paw or two hanging over the edge. Cracker liked to feel Willie's back against hers. She also liked it when he slept with his arms around her. Bliss.

On evenings of the three weekends they'd so far lived in this new place, Willie's parents let them sleep on the floor in the small front room that jutted out with windows on three sides. It was like floating in a boat through the apartments of Chicago. Cracker knew this because she and Willie had been on a boat together once. They'd both liked that. She liked water. She liked it at the lake, and she liked it in the bathtub. Willie started the water going. She didn't see why she couldn't get in the bath with Willie. She jumped halfway in the tub and licked Willie's face.

Willie heard his mom calling out, "Sweetheart, please don't let Cracker in the bathtub—her hair clogs the drain."

"Yeah, Mom!" He grunted as he pushed Cracker out of the tub. When she gave him a forlorn look, he said, "Maybe if my dad takes me to the Cubs game Saturday, Mom will take you out for a walk. But don't pull so hard on the leash." Willie knew that the Cubs weren't even in town this Saturday, but the lie made him feel better.

Cracker's ears perked up at the words "walk" and "leash," but she relaxed again as Willie kept talking. "If she doesn't take you out, I'll take you for an extra-long W-A-L-K when we get back." Cracker jumped up. She loved it when they went on a "double-you-ale-kay." That was the same as a "walk."

Willie dunked under the water with his eyes open, watching the ceiling waver. He stayed under until he couldn't hold his breath any longer. He was lying to her. By Saturday, Cracker would no longer be his dog. He'd begged everyone he knew, and his parents had even taken out a newspaper ad. But neither he nor his parents could find a new owner for Cracker. They'd taken her to the pound, but then when they got there, he couldn't give her up. The pound told him that she would probably end up getting put down. Hardly any of the dogs were adopted.

In the bathtub Willie came up for air. Cracker was licking one of her front paws. She'd been doing that ever since they moved to the apartment and she'd actually licked away a raw spot. That's how Willie knew Cracker was worried.

When Willie had checked his own newspaper ad, he'd noticed another. The U.S. Army needed German shepherds and Labs to go to Vietnam.

Willie hopped out of the tub and dried off. He pulled on his pajamas, and Cracker followed him into their bedroom. He didn't even call out good night to his parents, just shut the door and got in bed.

Willie pressed up against the wall, and Cracker stretched across the rest of the bed. He lay with his eyes open. Tomorrow Cracker would be on her way to dog-training school, and then to Vietnam, where she could serve her country, and—more importantly—live. Hopefully. *Live*.

Cracker sniffed at Willie as he drifted off. Something was wrong with him lately. He was acting funny, and that made him smell a little different. Whatever was wrong with him made her feel kind of sad. She stood up on the bed and pushed her nose onto his cheek, then lifted her nose a bit and sniffed at him. She did smell a little bloody spot on his knee, but she didn't think that was what was bothering him. She lay down lethargically. Whenever Willie didn't feel good, she didn't feel good either.

Cracker opened her eyes when Willie's parents walked into the room. She thought they were going to scold her, as they sometimes did, for taking up so much space or for being wet. Or something. Except for scolding, they hardly ever paid much attention to her. Now they petted her head and scratched her ears and called her "good girl" over and over. That was nice. Weird, but nice. Then they left. Cracker stared a moment at the crack of light under the door. She felt even more disturbed than before. She licked her paw for a while. But Willie was here and everything was peaceful, and so finally, she fell asleep.

In the morning, as always, Willie rushed around

the apartment. He fed Cracker, took her out to run a few times up and down the alley, took her home, and changed her water. Then, instead of running out the front door with his books, he threw his arms around Cracker's neck and hugged her so hard, she squirmed and had to pull away.

Willie's mother hovered over them. Cracker whined, completely confused. "Willie, you poor thing," said Willie's mother. "Why don't you stay home today?"

"I can't watch," he said. "I don't want to watch them take her."

Cracker pawed at his shirt so hard, her nails ripped through the material. *Uh-oh.* She didn't move for a moment. But nobody scolded her. Things had gotten really weird around here.

Willie took her face in his hands and said, "Bye, Cracker. You're going to be the best dog in Vietnam!"

Then he ran out the front door with his books. When Willie hurried down the sidewalk in the mornings, Cracker liked to watch from the third-floor window in the boat room. She always felt the same sadness and slight sense of abandonment. Today she yelped at him as she watched his back. Instead of turning around, he started to run. She yelped more. Willie didn't even stop to wave before turning the corner and going wherever he was going. He'd always waved before.

His mother petted her more than she ever had before. A lot of time passed before she said, "You're a wonderful dog." Cracker whined and felt the urge to lick her raw spot. Then his mother left for wherever it was that she went all day. After everybody had gone, Cracker always just lay around the apartment. Her biggest decisions were whether to sleep in the bedroom or the boat room (she wasn't allowed in the living room) and whether to sneak a pee somewhere that Willie's parents wouldn't find it (she did this only once, but she thought about it a lot).

On this particular day Cracker decided (1) not to sneak a pee that morning and (2) to sleep in the bedroom. Willie would be gone for a while, so she made herself comfortable. For some reason, he always pulled the sheets and covers evenly over the bed before he left. It wasn't comfortable that way. Before she lay down, Cracker pawed and pawed at the covers until they were perfectly scrunched up in the middle. She snuggled into the covers and fell asleep.

She lifted up her head when she heard Willie's parents come home and a strange man talking with them. That was odd, but Cracker was only mildly interested. She was Willie's, and Willie was hers, and nothing else much mattered.

She started getting more interested—a lot more interested—when Willie's father walked into the bedroom carrying a leash and a leather contraption. This was not usual procedure; still, Cracker had learned to tolerate Willie's parents, even listen to them. A couple of times Willie's father had taken her to a place where a man poked and prodded her. So when the leather slipped over her nose, she didn't growl at all, or even protest. The leather prevented her from opening her mouth wide enough to bite. She *could* have knocked Willie's father right to the ground—and, actually, the thought did flash through her head—but she rejected that possibility pretty quickly. Even when he slipped a chain around her neck and pulled it tight, she figured he might be taking her to that place where she would be poked and prodded. Something felt wrong, but she basically trusted Willie's father.

When they reached the living room, however, Cracker saw a stranger in a uniform, and she smelled something uneasy in the air. People smelled different, acted different, looked different, and just plain *were* different when they felt uneasy. Willie's mother was crying. Willie's father and the man in uniform looked at the ground. Cracker was stronger than

Willie's father as well as stronger than the new man. She was probably stronger, and definitely faster, than both of them put together. She didn't like the way this new man smelled. She started to snarl. That always scared people. She tried to open her mouth and then snarled even louder.

Willie's father responded by handing the leash to the man in uniform. He cooed, "Nice dog. Good girl, Cracker." She snarled again and began to lunge at the man, who jerked hard on her chain. Cracker heard a very uncourageous squeal from her own throat. She tried to pull away, but the man jerked back even harder this time, and the same squeal involuntarily jumped from Cracker's throat. The funny thing was that the man didn't seem mean, just firm. He said, "Sit! No! Sit!" Finally, Cracker sat. The man looked at Willie's parents and said, "She'll do well in Vietnam."

"Thanks for packing her up for us," said Willie's mother. "We just couldn't bear to do it ourselves."

Willie's father said, "She's smart as the dickens. Stubborn, though. She and Willie flunked out of obedience school twice—she needs a good handler to really teach her right. She's strong, too. Feel her muscles." Willie's father reached down to squeeze one of her legs.

"I'll take your word for it," the man said. "Don't worry. The army will take good care of her."

Willie's father said, "Good luck, Crack."

The man laid a hand on the front doorknob. Cracker knew she shouldn't have let Willie's father put the chain and leather on her. She trusted Willie's parents only because they were Willie's parents, but she trusted Willie because, well, because he was Willie. He would help her as soon as he got home. The man took his hand off the doorknob and shook hands with Willie's father. "Let your son know she'll do fine." Cracker could see he was planning to take her somewhere now. She growled and started to leap at him. The man jerked the chain upward, briefly hanging Cracker in the air. She felt her throat constrict, and for a moment everything went black.

Two

WILLIE LOOKED UP AT THE THIRD-FLOOR WINDOW where he always saw Cracker waiting for him. He gasped when he saw that Cracker wasn't there. That might mean they'd already taken her. She had ESP, so she always knew when he was coming home, even when he was early. He started to trot. He'd probably get in trouble the next day for the way he'd jumped up from his desk and run from the classroom, but his parents could write a letter making up some excuse.

Willie called out to the closed window: "Cracker! Cra-a-a-acker!" She didn't appear, and Willie broke into a sprint.

He ran up his apartment steps two at a time. When he burst inside, he was already calling out,

"Cracker!" He stopped with just one foot inside the apartment. The other foot forgot to move.

There was Cracker, wearing a muzzle, and there were both his parents, and there was a man in uniform holding a leash that was attached to Cracker. Fury overcame Willie. "Let go of her!" he shouted.

His mother and father stared at him. Then his mother said, "You're home," as if his being home were the odd thing and not the man in uniform holding the leash that was attached to Cracker.

Willie looked accusingly at the man. "What are you doing?" Now his other foot remembered to move. He walked right up to the man and demanded, "Give me that leash." He put both hands around the leash.

Cracker came to life, growling at the man.

Willie's father grabbed hold of Willie's wrists.

"Willie. Please." He added, "You're making it harder on the dog."

Willie's mother said, "Sweetheart," and she reached out to pull him to her, but he shrugged her off. "Sweetheart, Cracker will be a war hero! Remember when we watched the news that night? The war dogs of Vietnam! You said it was neat!" She smiled, but Willie could see that her smile was phony.

"Mom, please!" Willie cried out.

Willie tried to grab the leash again while Cracker strained toward him. Willie's father held him back and said, "Willie, you have to think about Cracker for a minute. Look how upset you're making her."

And, indeed, Willie saw the desperation in Cracker's eyes. He had made her terrified. So he stepped back and whispered, "Bye, Cracker."

The man pulled as Cracker struggled. "Heel!" the man said. The last thing Willie saw was a glimpse of her frightened brown eyes, and then the door closed. He ran to the window and stared as Cracker and the man left the building. Cracker looked up at him before the man tore off the leather contraption and loaded her into a crate in the back of a van. When the van drove off, Willie watched until he couldn't see it anymore.

He didn't cry at all. It was just . . . the whole world was completely different now. It didn't matter if the Cubs won or lost, it didn't matter if his father had a job or not, and it didn't matter if he ever went back to school. The thought occurred to him that he should have cut off the hair at the tip of Cracker's tail or her nails or something so he could always have a piece of her. It was crazy, but he felt like he would give anything in the world for one of her toenails.

Three

CRACKER HAD STARTED LIFE OUT AS A BIG DEAL. She was born the daughter of Champion Felix Olympus von Braun, who a lot of people thought was one of the finest German shepherds ever bred. Olympus had won forty-seven Best of Show titles before his owners decided to retire him. Cracker's mother, Champion Midnight Moon of Shreveport, won seventeen Best of Shows, even beating Olympus one time. Cracker's name as a puppy was not Cracker, but Magnificent Dawn of Venus. Venus was expected to be a champion herself, for a lot of people thought she was the finest bitch in her litter. She was purchased for $1,500 by Willie's uncle on Willie's father's side and lived a pampered but lonely life in a big kennel with a big dog run.

She won Best Puppy in Match three times, even beating out her littermates.

But one day her left hind leg got caught on a piece of chain link in her day kennel, and the bone broke in two. After healing, she could still walk fine, but her leg bent in a certain way that made it impossible for her ever to be a great show dog. Willie's uncle decided to give her to Willie as a birthday present.

She was six months old. Willie named her Firecracker, and when he got her home, she immediately proceeded to figure out how to open the refrigerator, eating every piece of meat in there until her stomach was so swollen, she couldn't move. His parents had worried that she might need to go to the veterinarian and have the food surgically removed from her stomach. But Willie just hauled her onto his bed and let her spread out while he squished himself up against the wall.

When she woke up, he was sleeping with his arms around her. At first she growled, but then she realized she liked the feeling. Despite the attention that had been showered on her previously, she'd never quite felt loved in this way before. And so she began a life of being pampered in a different way. Willie worshipped her. Oh, he taught her a lot of stuff and made her behave sometimes, but she knew she had the upper hand. She was born to be a beloved queen and eat good snacks.

So why was she now trapped in a crate in the back of a van? Why were two other dogs who looked like her also trapped in crates in the back of the van? She howled. The howling reverberated in her ears and seemed to fill the whole world. The other dogs seemed scared, but they didn't howl. Cracker concentrated on Willie as she howled. Maybe he didn't understand the seriousness of the situation. Where was he? It was getting dark already. It was time for their walk.

She was so lost in her howling that she didn't have the slightest idea how much time had elapsed by the time the truck stopped. The two men carried out the other dogs one at a time. She breathed deeply and howled even louder. As soon as the two men returned, she stopped howling and tensed her body.

"Beautiful animal," said one of the men.

"If you like dogs," said the other. He looked at her. "Dog, you're going to Vietnam. They got dog diseases there I can't even pronounce." He turned to the other man. "She'll be lucky to make it home in one piece."

"Actually, they keep the dogs there until they die," the other man said. "They never come home."

"No kidding? My dad had a Doberman who served in World War II, and he came back. He was the family dog after the war."

"They changed the policy with this war. The military considers the dogs equipment, and equipment is expendable."

Cracker growled as they neared the crate. They picked it up. She threw herself against the side of the crate and felt gratified when one of the men almost lost his balance. But it didn't stop the men from loading her into a big, dark room full of stifling air. She smelled more dogs and heard a couple of them howling. The room jerked, a whistle blew, and then the room jerked again and started moving. She couldn't see anything except a dark wall. This all went on so long that she fell asleep, dreaming of biting the man who had taken her from Willie.

When she woke up, the train had stopped. A voice from a loudspeaker boomed, "Lackland Air Force Base, ladies and gentlemen." But all she could see was the wall.

Two new men picked up her crate and took it to a place that was almost like the place Willie's father had taken her a couple of times. A man put a new leather contraption around her snout so she couldn't open her mouth, and then another man poked and prodded her. So maybe she was at a similar place as before, and Willie's father might come get her before long. The man tried to grab her neck, but she whirled around and threw herself as hard as she could against him. She heard his head clunk and felt satisfied. Then another man came and grabbed the chain around her neck and held her down while the first man stuck her with a needle.

After that, the days were filled with odd activities. Men would make loud noises around her and study her reaction. A big, whirring mechanical thing some-one called "chopper" landed nearby. Again men poked and prodded her. One man examined the leg she'd broken by pressing his fingers into it.

Then one day a woman came along and stuck her with yet another needle. The woman had kind eyes. "You passed all the tests, Cracker. We need to tattoo your ear, baby. Go to sleep, sweetheart. Sleepytimes."

And that was the last thing Cracker remembered until she woke up in another big, dark, rumbling room, just like the previous big, dark, rumbling room. For some reason, her right ear hurt, as if it were scratched. That made her start up a new howl, and what she heard in reply surprised her: There must have been twenty other dogs, all howling or whimpering. They kept it up as long as they could, and then they all slept. She usually didn't care for other dogs but she already felt a sense of kinship with these. What was happening to them? The room stopped again. She stayed still to concentrate on the commotion behind her, and then two new men were carrying her crate out of the room and to the back of a truck. She knew what a truck was. She'd ridden in trucks with Willie when they went camping a couple of times. The air outside was warm, humid, and fresh, and the pain in her ear had subsided a little. Another dog looked at her, which annoyed her, so she snarled and threw herself against the side of the cage. He whimpered. *Annoying coward!* She met eyes with yet another dog, one even bigger than her. He didn't annoy her. They looked at each other, and she felt a mutual respect. She pushed her nose to the gate of her crate, and he did the same in his crate.

When the truck stopped, several men in uniforms crowded around the back talking with the drivers. The uniforms were the same as the one worn by the man who took her from Willie.

"A couple of them are real beauties," the driver said. "That one's big for a female."

"How much does she weigh?"

The driver looked at a clipboard. "Hundred and ten. Moderately aggressive, just what the army is looking for. She had a broken leg, but they're keeping her anyway. Never heard of that."

Another couple of men lifted down her crate, and she lunged at the side. These men weren't thrown off balance, though.

"She seems more than moderately aggressive," said the driver. "Gorgeous animal, though. From Chicago. Name's Cracker."

At the sound of her name Cracker's ears perked up, but nobody said anything more to her. From the truck, she smelled grass and lots of different people.

The dog crates were carried to a nearby kennel area. One by one the dogs were taken out of the crates and put into a kennel. Only Cracker waited in her crate. Finally, a man appeared with padding on his arms, and he and another man pulled Cracker out of her crate and tried to push her into a kennel. She slammed her body into the padded man and heard that wonderful *clunk* noise as his head hit the concrete. She saw one of his legs rise as he fell.

A third man appeared from somewhere and reached for the back of her neck. She figured whatever he wanted to do was bad, so she heaved her side into him, and he ended up grabbing her around the stomach. They wrestled and wrestled.

"Throw her in the kennel!" somebody yelled. She bit the third man's arm.

"Ahhh! Ahhh! Crazy dog!" Suddenly, the man let go of her, and the three men rushed *into* her kennel and slammed the door. Cracker looked at them. They looked at her. Even she knew this was all wrong. *Oh, well.* She trotted off but stopped when she saw another man wrapped in padding.

"You're supposed to grab them by the back of the neck!" shouted one of the men in the kennel. But as the man moved toward her, she easily galloped away. She kept running until she came to a long building. She turned around and saw what was now six men closing in on her, breathing hard.

For a while she ran in a big circle as she listened to the men losing their breath. She heard one of them trip; ordinarily, this might have been fun. But there was nowhere to go. And there was no Willie to go to. This wasn't fun at all. So she ran back to the only place she knew of where she might belong: the kennel. The gate was open, and she slipped in. It took the men a couple of minutes to reach the gate and slam it shut.

They looked at her. She looked at them. Then

nothing happened. She turned her head both ways and saw that kennels with dogs stretched into the distance on both sides of her. Two kennels down was the dog she thought was okay. They met eyes. He looked a little scared—but a little happy, too—to see her. The dog to her right was half her size. She wagged her tail eagerly. Cracker went to sniff noses with her. Then Cracker waved her tail in approval.

A roof protected one section of her kennel from the sun, and a bowl of water sat in a corner. She lapped eagerly at the water. The dog to the left of her whined and pawed at her kennel. She growled, and the dog slunk back. Some dogs she just didn't like.

The men still watched Cracker as she lay down. And then they left, and she waited and waited and waited, occasionally chewing on the steel gate or licking her raw spot.

She felt crazy in this kennel, but at the same time she knew that there was nowhere else to go. She tried to feel exactly where Willie was. She knew the direction, and she knew he was far, but that was it. She whined and laid her head on her paws.

But the more she waited, the sadder she felt. And then the sadder she felt, the angrier she felt at everybody who came by. Whenever someone tried to take her out, she growled with such menace that they left her and took out another dog instead. She bit a fellow who brought her food in, just because he annoyed her. She felt furious with everybody, even the people who just walked in front of her cage.

The dog on her right, the one everyone called "Tristie," had guys petting her and taking her out all the time. Everybody liked Tristie, even Cracker. Sometimes Tristie would slap a paw on the fencing between them, and Cracker would slap a paw in the same place. Then they would run up and down their kennels at the same time. Other times, when Tristie was away, Cracker would lie sullenly at the back of her kennel. One day two men in uniform stood in front of her cage. She snarled and jumped over and over at the gate. She hated them—whoever they were.

"This one's not going to make it. She's too mean. They're going to have to put her down or maybe make her a sentry dog."

"Five dollars says she makes it."

They shook hands.

Four

RICK HANSKI WAS GOING TO WHIP THE WORLD. It was just a feeling he had. He hadn't done much to back up this idea, but he just knew it. He'd signed up for the army on his seventeenth birthday, after a long talk with his parents and grandparents about his future and about his father's hardware store and who might take it over someday if not him. His parents were first-generation Scandinavian Americans—all four of his grandparents came from the tundra. After he'd moved to Wisconsin, Grandpa Hanski had gotten a patent for a bar clamp and sold the patent to a big tool company. He'd used the money to start a hardware store that Rick's father had inherited when Grandpa retired early. Rick had worked at the store since he was a kid.

When he wanted to relax, he liked to make things: He'd made quite a few frames for his mother and a couple of chairs for his father. He liked to shape things. But he knew his work wasn't good enough to sell, and anyway, making stuff was mostly just for relaxing. It took his mind off of what worries he had. He guessed his biggest worry was that he wasn't sure he wanted to take over the hardware store someday. Everybody had assumed that the store was his future; that's why his parents didn't complain about his so-so grades. They were just proud that he worked hard in the store, and they'd never made him feel bad that his sister, Amy, was a math prodigy who'd graduated from MIT a couple of years ago and was now going for her PhD in Applied Mathematics, whatever that meant. He did overhear his father saying once that his sister had a calling, whereas Rick was a "good, strong, well-mannered boy," just like all the Hanski men had been at his age.

When his father had met one of the actual DeWalts at a convention once, he'd talked about it for days, as if he'd met the president or something. But sometimes, working at the hardware store, Rick felt . . . not bored exactly, but like something wasn't quite right. And Rick was filled with guilt, because he knew how proud his father was of the store. But it just didn't feel right for him. So when Rick turned seventeen, he thought he'd sign up like some of the other local guys had. He was a man now, not a boy, no matter what his parents thought. He'd made the announcement at dinner the week before he turned seventeen. Everyone had just finished eating.

Rick had turned to his father, who Rick could tell was just about to stand up.

"Dad?"

"Hmm?"

"I'd like to sign up."

"Sign up for what?"

Rick had felt four sets of eyes burn into him. His parents' and grandparents'. They'd probably been thinking dinner was over, and it was time to watch television, maybe laugh at a TV comedy. Life didn't hold many surprises in the Hanski household. "Sign up for Vietnam. But I need you to approve since I'll be only seventeen."

Rick felt his own chest heaving with nervousness but kept his eyes trained on his father's. Then everybody was talking at once. His parents and grandparents grilled him for hours. He'd prepared for all this, had planned to start out by talking about something he'd done once: save a kid's life. It was a couple of years ago, and he'd been standing on a sidewalk and seen a six-year-old boy run into the path of an oncoming bus. Rick had pushed the boy out of the way and just managed to get out of the way himself. Those moments stood out with clarity in Rick's mind, whereas every day at the hardware store dulled in comparison. That's what he'd wanted to talk about that night. But instead, his family had hardly given him a chance to speak.

They'd lectured him about what he planned to do when he got back, about whether he really understood that war was an "ugly thing," as his grandfather said over and over. Grandpa had lived in Finland during World War II. He *knew* war.

"I know, Grandpa," Rick started to say, but then his grandmother broke in.

"If we'd pushed him more in school, maybe none of this would be happening," Grandma Hanski had said. If they'd pushed him in school, she continued, maybe he'd want to go to college and be an accountant for the hardware store or something. Finally, at the end of the four hours, silence fell and everybody turned to Rick's father. His father was a serious man who surprised you sometimes with a practical joke or a belly laugh. But there had been no joking at that table for those four hours.

His father had leaned his forehead on his finger-
tips in deep thought. Then he'd raised his head and
nodded and said, "You do what you have to do."
His father came with him to sign the papers, and the
Saturday before Rick left, his family threw a big
party. A lot of their friends were also customers.
Farmers, furniture makers, factory workers. A couple
of the old men had played saws with violin bows.
Lots of laughing, a little crying.

And now Rick Hanski was going to whip the
world. That's what he thought to himself as he
walked across the lush grass at Fort Benning. He'd
always been self-confident. Working with your tools
did that to you, made you see how you could shape
things. He had to admit that so far he hadn't been a
resounding success in the army. He'd gotten written
up during basic training for "lack of tact and diplomacy." Apparently, some of the mucky-mucks
thought he was too outspoken. Originally what had
happened was that a sergeant had demanded a loan
of ten dollars for a poker game. *Demanded* it. Rick
had said politely, "I'm sorry. Don't have it, Sarge."
The next time the sergeant saw him, he'd demanded
ten dollars again, and that had just offended Rick's
sense of fairness. In the house in which he'd been
raised, the world was a fair place. Maybe Rick had

always been a bit of a firebrand—got that from his mother's father. His mother said it wasn't a bad temper, it was "righteous indignation." Whatever it was, it didn't get you far in the army. Then, in advanced infantry training, Rick had gotten into a couple of fistfights—more righteous indignation—that got him written up.

Rick had to admit that a couple of times he'd lain on his cot and wondered whether he'd made a mistake by signing up. He was proud of his sister, but maybe her brains were part of the problem. Rick didn't like to admit that. He wasn't jealous really. He was proud of her. He just smarted a little from it all. He still remembered something a math teacher had told him. This was way back in seventh grade, right as he was leaving class with a C minus on a test. His teacher had said, "You're a generalist, Richard. Some people like your sister are born to be specialists. Others are born to be generalists, even if they apply themselves . . . which you don't." Actually, he'd studied hard for that test. Then his teacher had mussed his hair. "You're a nice boy." She was an old lady—must've been fifty-five at least, and he'd been self-confident even then. But something about the word "generalist" got to him and bothered him still.

At the time, that righteous indignation had risen in him, and he'd said coolly, "Can I go now, ma'am?"

Saving that boy's life was the one resounding success of Rick's life. And he wasn't even sure what "apply yourself" meant. It sounded like gluing yourself to drywall or something.

Anyway, despite the bad write-ups in his file, his best friend's older brother, who'd flown through Officer Candidate School the previous year and also happened to be good friends with the man in charge of dog-handler training, had put in a good word for Rick, and he was offered the chance to become a dog handler in Vietnam. There was a shortage of dog handlers and they were in demand. Becoming a dog handler meant extra training, and the more training you had, the longer it would take you to get to Nam for your yearlong tour in country. Originally, Rick had wanted to get in country as soon as possible, but he'd decided that while he still planned to whip the world, there was nothing wrong with delaying the timing. So Rick figured he would still whip the world, but with a dog at his side. Although his was one of the few families in the community without a dog, all his friends owned dogs, and Rick had always liked them fine.

He walked across the field toward the kennels. The humidity felt like a hand or somebody with a fever hovering very close to his face but not quite touching it. A lot of guys were complaining about the unusually hot weather today. But the way Rick figured it, if a little humidity could stop you from whipping the world, well, you might as well be a bookkeeper for a hardware store. He'd just been assigned the dog he would train with. The sarge had snickered when he assigned Rick to what was supposedly one of the biggest, and apparently meanest, dogs in the kennel. She'd tussled with or bitten several personnel already. Rick knew the sarge didn't like him because of the aforementioned lack of tact and diplomacy recorded in his file. Sometimes Rick wondered whether he should have listened to his uncle in California—when his uncle had heard Rick wanted to join the army, he had offered to take Rick in and turn him into a master carpenter. But you weren't going to save any lives by pounding nails.

Rick stopped in front of a cage reading CRACKER. She was big, but she looked docile enough, lying on the concrete with her front paws delicately crossed. Rick didn't feel a lick of fear.

Her kennel was next to Tristie's—one of the two

dogs everybody somehow knew were already excellently trained. Rick knew that Tristie had been assigned a handler nicknamed "Twenty-Twenty." He actually had 20/40 vision, but he had this weird habit of always doing eye exercises, rolling his eyes around or moving them left and right as far as he could. Then he would lie on the ground with his palms covering his eyes. Some of the guys thought he was nuts, especially since he was black and didn't talk or act the way some people seemed to think black people should. But Rick thought he was okay. He stopped to pat Tristie. Tristie was unnaturally skinny—you could see her ribs sticking out—but very energetic and smart. She must have weighed less than half of what Cracker weighed, but Rick would have liked pulling her.

He didn't open Cracker's cage just yet. He looked at the rows of German shepherds and shepherd mixes. Apparently, Fort Benning, Georgia, housed hundreds of potential scout dogs. This row housed the dogs who would be traveling to Vietnam with his platoon. All these dogs at Benning, and he'd pulled one with an attitude. Rick wondered where the other dogs were housed. He'd heard Fort Benning was almost as big as New York City's five boroughs, but Rick had no idea what shape it was.

As a matter of fact, he didn't even know what a "borough" was. Fort Benning was the center of army training. Among other things, it housed Officer Candidate School, jump—or parachute—school, basic training, and Special Forces. Rick just leaned on the cage, thinking idly about jump school.

Cracker didn't even move her eyes as the man laid a palm on her gate, but she growled, still without looking at him.

"Cracker!" he said. "Hey, girl! Cracker!" Cracker listened to him but didn't move her head. Finally, she moved just her eyes in his direction. He reached a forefinger in and wiggled it. *Obviously an idiot.* She didn't bother to raise her head. He started to open the gate while she lay still but tensed slightly. Then he cracked the gate open a touch, and she lunged.

He slammed the gate shut as her body hit the wire. Though he stood safely outside the gate, he took a step back. That seemed to satisfy her a bit, but she didn't move from the gate. *Wow.* What was her problem? Rick had never seen a dog move so fast. He noticed that some guys had gathered at the end of the kennels watching him. He hoped he looked convincingly nonchalant.

All right. So. Maybe this would be a little tougher than he'd thought, but she was just a dog,

right? And he was a human. He was superior,
right?

He reached into his pocket and took out his
secret weapon: a wiener.

"Wiener?" he said in a low voice. According to
the manual, the men weren't supposed to give the
dogs treats. First of all, the dogs needed to stay lean
and muscular for the hard work they'd be doing in
Vietnam. Second of all, the dogs were supposed to
follow their handlers' directions out of love for the
person, not out of love for treats. But this was a
special situation.

He saw Cracker eyeing the wiener. "Wiener?" he
said again.

Cracker paused. She knew that word: "wiener."
Willie had used that word. She hadn't seen Willie
for a long time. But she remembered him, the way
he smelled, the way he breathed, the way his arms
felt wrapped around her. She also remembered
wieners. Wieners smelled good. Very good. She
stopped growling but didn't relax her body.

"Wiener for Cracker?"

Everybody in the world seemed to know her name,
even this man with a wiener. He opened the gate very
slowly and broke off a piece of wiener. Cracker
growled. What did this man want? He threw her the

piece of wiener. She let it fall to the ground before sniffing it suspiciously, keeping her eyes on the man the whole time. Then she snapped up the meat and hopped backward. The man didn't move. *Mmmmm. Good wiener.* Not that she'd ever tasted a bad one.

"Wiener?" said the man. "Another wiener for Cracker?"

Mmmm. Wiener for Cracker. He pushed the gate open farther. She moved back rather than lunging. But she stayed poised for lunging. She didn't growl, however. The man opened his hand, and inside was another small piece of wiener. She stood still but wouldn't move toward him.

He sat down in the doorway. "Okay, have it your way." He laid the wiener bit on the ground before him. She just sat and looked at him, not at the wiener. He laid another piece of wiener down.

She lunged suddenly, causing him to scramble up, but she wasn't lunging for him. She snapped up the two wiener bits. Then she stood growling, her whole body tense, in case she needed to rip his face off.

Rick's heart was pounding. She was like a cat. He considered himself pretty quick, yet she'd caught him by surprise. Still, he knew she could have bitten him if she'd wanted. So he must have made *some* progress.

He held out his open palms to her. She sniffed his hands. She sat. Sitting was the universal language for, *I'll take another wiener.*

She stiffened as he moved his fingers under her chin. What was the point of that? Then he moved his hand up and scratched behind her ear.

"Good girl." He patted his own head. "Rick."

Good girl. Hmmmm. He scratched her other ear. Cracker liked "good girl." When Willie said it, it was even better than "wiener," though not by much. She missed "good girl." Thinking of Willie made her whine.

The man's hands were firmer and bigger than Willie's, and his smell was stronger, sweatier. But he smelled okay. He rubbed her head in a new way that she liked, pressing all his fingers at once onto her skull. He did this for quite a while before he said, "Good girl!" and left.

Rick stepped outside, mentally patting himself on the back. He was still going to whip the world, no doubt about it.

Another man—a tall, friendly guy named Cody Willis—leaned toward Cracker's kennel and said, "Good girl."

"Hey, you're not supposed to do that," Rick said.

"Do what?"

"Once you get a dog, you're only supposed to praise your own dog. Nobody can praise anybody else's dog. It's in the manual." The dogs were supposed to bond with one man and one man only. On the other hand, the manual also said that if a dog's handler got wounded, sometimes the dogs felt so protective of their handler that they wouldn't let the medic near enough to help. In that case, someone was supposed to shoot the dog. So it was good for the dog to at least be able to tolerate someone else besides the handler.

Cody shrugged good-naturedly. "Okay, man." He gestured toward a huge, calm dog. "I pulled Bruno."

That feeling passed through Rick, that feeling of smarting that he got every so often when people talked about what a genius his sister was. Not envy, though, just a stinging sensation. Everybody knew that Bruno was a smart, strong dog, and friendly, too. Some of the guys had taken him out and found he was perfectly trained already. He was older than the others—four and a half years old—but apparently such a good dog that the army had kept him. In fact, Bruno had almost been stationed at Lackland because one of the captains had taken a shine to him. But the captain had gotten appendicitis and Bruno ended up here after all, to get assigned to some teacher's pet like Cody.

Rick leaned in toward Cracker. "Remember. Rick." He started walking away, but the Hanski good manners kicked in, and he turned and said to Cody, "Bruno's a great dog. Congratulations." *Then* he left.

Cracker sat at the gate as the man walked away. She liked "good girl." And the man was okay. But he'd forgotten to give her the rest of the wiener. Tristie came to the fence and sniffed at her.

That night as the moon rose over the trees in the distance, Cracker actually lifted her head every so often when she heard an unusual sound. And a couple of times she sniffed the air with interest. She hadn't felt interested in smells or sounds for a long time. They seemed a little more intriguing tonight, but she still felt a hurt inside of herself that wouldn't go away. A huge bird sailed across the sky, and she barked at it. A number of other dogs also barked. *Wow.* Cracker had forgotten how good it felt to bark at a bird like that. She stretched her muscles and looked around, then paced back and forth a few times before settling down for bed.

She slept intermittently through the night, occasionally hearing what sounded like firecrackers in the distance. She knew what firecrackers were, because Willie had taken her to a park a few times to watch the exploding lights in the sky. She'd heard firecracker noises many times since she'd been in this cage, but tonight, for some reason, she raised her ears and sniffed the air.

In the morning, the man with strong hands showed up again, this time with dog food. She could smell him coming before she could see him. When he arrived, he opened the gate and set down the food. She paused for just a moment. What, no *wiener*? It didn't appear, so she ate the food. *Not bad.*

"I'm Rick," said the man. He scratched her and said "good girl" a few times. He looked at the inside of her ear and said, "Seventy-two-A-O. That's your number. I got a number too, on my dog tag. I don't need a tattoo in my ear like you." He'd heard that a lot of good handlers talked to their dogs kind of like they were people. It felt a little peculiar, but she seemed to like it.

"Woof!" she said. She sent the thought at him: *Give me a wiener.* She sat, and there it was in his hand, a piece of wiener. She gobbled it up.

He lowered his voice. "We're not supposed to give you treats. Don't tell anyone. Good girl. Come!"

Then he pulled the chain around her throat, choking her a bit. She growled and tensed: She might need to rip his face off after all. She saw other men pulling their dogs. One dog dragged all four of his paws on the ground as the man holding his leash kept saying, "Heel! No! Heel!" Cracker tried to tug in the opposite direction, but Rick jerked the chain firmly.

"No!" he said.

She knew "no," but she'd never heard it said quite so firmly before. Willie's father said it angrily sometimes, and Willie said it lovingly, like he didn't mean it. Rick said it firmly, and he meant it.

Rick walked her along with the other dogs, but she didn't heel—she either lagged or pulled. A slight drizzle fell on them. Rick saw Cody jerk expertly on Bruno's leash and say, "Heel!" Bruno heeled perfectly at Cody's left side. Rick said, "Heel!" and Cracker sat down instead. Rick said to Cody, "I don't think this dog is gonna learn so easy."

Cody turned to Rick and said, "Want me to give it a try?"

"Okay, but it won't make a difference." Rick knew dogs. Even if he'd never had one, he'd been around them all his life.

Cody handed Bruno's leash to Rick. Bruno sat patiently. *What a dog!* Rick felt the sting again. Then he watched Cody slap his left leg, step out with his left leg, and snap, "Heel!" to Cracker. Cracker heeled perfectly, even when Cody went in circles or trotted. They trotted back, and Cody and

Rick traded leashes. "She's already trained," Cody said. "And very well."

Rick looked at Cracker and mumbled, "Okay, no more games." Rick imitated Cody, but Cracker started to drag her legs like the other dog had. So he had no choice but to drag her to formation like a fool.

Cody walked beside them with Bruno, the Mr. Universe of dogs. Cody half grinned the whole time. He was six feet four—a full half foot taller than Rick—but weighed only about three pounds more. He liked to say he was the skinniest man in Minnesota. Cody's eyes were the blue of a lighter flame, his expression gullible. He had a slight overbite. He was the most cheerful man Rick had ever met. He smiled about everything, especially eating. Rick was a happy enough guy, but he certainly wasn't cheerful. Cheerful was, well, not really in keeping with the Hanski idea of manhood. Certainly Rick believed that the cup was always half full, but this guy seemed to think it was overflowing.

"You never had a dog?" Cody said now.

"A bunch of my friends did," Rick said defensively. But he added, "You?"

"Got a collie now. Looks just like Lassie. Had dogs all my life."

All the dogs lined up with the platoon, which was broken up into three squads of eight men each. The sergeant stood in front and announced, "The first part of this course consists of basic dog training: sit, stay, heel, down, and come." U-Haul met every cliché of a sergeant. He was big, mean, loud, and insulting. He acted a lot the way the sergeant during basic training had. Rick wondered if they'd all watched a training film on how to act like a big, mean, loud, insulting sergeant.

In the advanced infantry training Rick had gone through just before dog training, the sarge didn't insult them much. Counting basic, AIT, and now dog training, Rick figured he might end up spending as much time training as fighting.

"Are—you—listening—soldier?!" U-Haul was staring straight at him.

Rick said, "Yes, sir!" That had slipped out. He knew exactly what U-Haul would answer.

U-Haul put his face a few inches from Rick's. "I work for a living. Don't ever call me 'sir' again."

"Yes, Sergeant."

U-Haul stomped down the row. "You are the boss, men!" he shouted. "Do not take anything from your dog. You are in control. Your dog is eager to please you, for that is a dog's mission in life. Don't ever give your dog treats." Rick's eyes flicked down toward Cracker, as though she might give him away. "Your dog works for love of man, not for love of food." He looked right at Rick, as if he knew Rick had given Cracker wieners. Rick didn't change expressions, and the sarge continued. "The basis of all our training is obedience and the bond between man and dog. At the end of training the best handlers will receive trophies."

Starting that day, and for day after day after day, all they ever did, it seemed to Cracker, was sit, stay, and heel in every direction, including in circles. Sometimes she knew what Rick was going to say before he spoke, so she did it before he asked, and he would pull at her neck and say, "No!" Then he would tell her to do what she'd just done. She figured he was kind of mixed up that way. Sometimes she did something totally different from what he'd asked, just to annoy him.

Rick found that Cody was right, that Cracker obviously had learned all this earlier. Still, after a while, whenever Rick told her to sit, she sometimes liked to glare at him first and *then* sit. Rick figured this was to let him know that she understood the power of the chain around her neck, but *he* had better understand that she knew the chain was the only reason she needed to listen to him. If she hesitated too long, he'd jerk the chain and say, "No! Sit!" and she'd sit, but with a glare in her eyes.

One morning in formation she simply refused to sit. The entire platoon watched as Rick said over and over, "No! Sit!" and pulled at her chain. Some guys were even laughing. Finally, he had to simultaneously push her butt down as hard as he could while pulling up on her chain until she sat. He looked straight ahead—no way was he going to look at the sergeant. But he thought, *I hate that man for assigning me this dog.* Rick had never hated anyone in his life. Every community had a couple of cranks who were just what they were, and you accepted that. But you didn't hate them. This was hate.

Sarge came up to him as if reading his mind and said, almost happily, "That was the most impressive example of incompetence I have seen in my entire career in the army." He turned to the other men.

Heeling was another problem. Half the time Rick was dragging Cracker or else she was pulling him. Meanwhile, Bruno walked obediently at the side of Cody. Tristie was the same: perfect. Rick had just got the wrong dog, that was the problem. This was the first dog he'd ever met who didn't seem crazy about him.

"I'm on to your ways," he said to her one morning. Whenever he lost his temper, his parents always tried to reason with him. Maybe that would work with a dog. "You're just like me. No tact and diplomacy because you think this is all unfair, right?" She looked at him without expression. They just weren't bonding at all. He took a breath and said, "All right, then. Come!" She sat.

After a while the dogs learned other commands at the obstacle course like "crawl" and "hup," which was the command used for both "jump up" and "jump down." Sometimes when Rick said "hup," Cracker ran around the obstacle instead of over it. Other times she did it perfectly. In the meantime, the squad moved on to hand signals and the dogs started to work more like teammates with their handlers. Rick and Cracker weren't the worst team in the squad, but they were definitely in the bottom 5 or 10 percent.

At night, if she bothered to think about it at all, Cracker would lie next to Tristie and she would know that things weren't going well. But she didn't know what the result of that would be. At Willie's once when she'd scratched a couch cover, Willie's parents made her stay outside for an hour. She knew it was an hour because Willie's father kept shouting over and over, "An hour outside! An hour outside!"

Anyway, even if she now kind of had a human who kind of seemed like he was hers, she also now knew that people just abandoned you eventually. It had already happened to her twice. So why listen to them? Why do what they say?

As for Rick, he would lie on his cot thinking about the day's various failures. His ego was taking quite a beating. All Rick could do was hold his head high, the way he'd been taught.

One night after an especially bad day of training, Rick lay in bed fuming and couldn't sleep. U-Haul had told him that they might cycle Cracker out or give her to another handler, if any wanted her. "Cycling out" could mean anything. It could mean returning her to civilian life, it could mean giving her to another handler, it could mean sending her to sentry training, and it could mean putting her down. Sarge said he didn't know what would become of her if she was cycled out.

Rick lay thinking about changing dogs and leaving Cracker to her fate. It wasn't personal against the dog or anything, but, after all, the right dog could save his life once he got to Vietnam. The wrong dog could get him killed. The only thing that was stopping him from letting Cracker go was when he thought about the two letters he'd already received from the boy who'd previously owned Cracker. Both letters asked if Cracker was the best dog in training and both talked about how much he still loved her. The boy claimed he'd taught Cracker ninety words. And Cody had told Rick he thought she was a great dog. But, dammit, Rick hated being one of the worst teams in class!

Rick swung up from his cot and walked outside into the mild night air. In the distance he saw some guys standing by a jeep. Fort Benning was mostly quiet at night, but some work had to be done at all hours. He jogged up to the jeep.

"Say, you guys heading toward the kennels?"

"Yeah, need a lift?"

"Thanks, man."

They drove quietly. When they arrived, one of the guys said, "We're returning in an hour. Need a lift back?"

"You guys are lifesavers."

"Cool. See ya then."

Cracker knew Rick was coming before he got there. She didn't move from her plywood bed, though. She felt kind of wary. This could be something bad. When he got to the gate, he softly called, "Cracker," but she still didn't move. And she could smell that he hadn't even brought a wiener. He opened the gate and said,

"Cracker! Come." She didn't move. It gave her pleasure not to move when he called.

He leaned his head against the kennel and didn't have a thought in the world about what he should do next. He didn't even understand why he'd come. Then he walked inside and knelt next to her plywood bed.

"I don't know," he said. "I don't know what to do. You tell me."

She didn't move.

He reached out to rub her head. God, she was a beautiful animal, maybe the best-looking dog in training. And the boy had claimed he'd taught her ninety words. She *had* to be smart if that was true. He looked around. The other dogs were stirring, and a couple had barked at him. "Cracker," he said. "Does it make a difference if you die without applying yourself? Like if you're dead, you're gone, so what's the difference if you applied yourself or not?"

Cracker just looked at him. She didn't know what any of those words meant except "dead." Willie had taught her that when she found the dead bird. He'd also taught her to play dead. Is that what he wanted?

"What am I doing talking to a dog at two in the morning?" Rick said. He must have lost his mind.

"Good girl!" He pointed to another tree and said, "Run to the tree!" She ran to the tree. "Good girl!" Then he directed her to run among a whole bunch of trees. And they heeled, sat, lay down, and did every single thing they'd been working on for weeks. When they were finished, she was panting but felt elated.

Rick felt elated too. He was also panting. He threw his arms around her. "Good girl," he said. "Good, good girl."

And for the first time since he'd ever said it, she knew he meant it. It made her feel wonderful.

Rick kenneled her and caught his ride back. Jeez, he couldn't believe this dog could have been put down.

After that night, training got better and better. In fact, Rick started lying in bed thinking about the day's triumphs instead of the day's failures. It didn't happen all at once, but after a while it seemed to Rick that they were in maybe the top 25 percent of the class. Not that this trophy business meant anything—they were all in this together. But there was nothing wrong with being the best.

Every day the instructor told the men the same thing: "When you get to Vietnam, you will do everything with your dog. Don't take a leak without your dog. Don't have a smoke without your dog. If you sneeze, I want that dog at your side. In Vietnam entire companies of men will rely on your dog to save their lives. But your dog isn't working for those companies, your dog is working for you. I want you to bond with that dog until you don't know where the dog ends and you begin!"

Rick had heard this twenty times already. Since that night running among the trees, he had started taking Cracker with him everywhere. It turned out she was a real people dog. She hated being alone, and he started to feel guilty when he did take a leak without her. Sometimes, even when he got leave and went into town, he would catch himself wondering what Cracker was doing.

Training was actually starting to get fun. Sometimes the platoon would go out on the road and jog with their dogs heeling at their sides. If they ran into civilians, the civilians always wanted to take pictures. One hot day they sweated down the road as a couple of gorgeous girls called out, "They're so cute!" The sarge halted the platoon so the girls could take pictures of the dogs. That gave all the guys new respect for their dogs: They were not only well-trained animals, they were outstanding girl-catchers.

Other times when a civilian wanted to take pictures, the sergeant would rage, "These dogs are not pets. These dogs are specialized military equipment."

Rick noticed that some of the dogs weren't as good in various ways as Tristie, Bruno, and—now—Cracker. One dog refused to jump over a wall when told. Another dog bit his handler several times. That dog finally got cycled out and went to wherever such dogs went, maybe to sentry dog training. They liked the dogs meaner there.

The more Rick trained, the more he started to feel that Cracker was reading his mind or something. Of course, he would never say this out loud, unless he wanted to be the laughingstock of the squad. In fact, when he first had the thought during formation one morning, he looked around self-consciously as if somebody might have read his mind.

Rick saw U-Haul scream at someone down the row and couldn't stifle a yawn. Suddenly, the sergeant marched right in front of Rick. Rick's heart raced. U-Haul had been looking another way, and Rick didn't see how he could have seen him yawn.

"You bored, Private?"

"No, SERGEANT!"

"No tact and diplomacy, is that correct, Private?"

"Yes, SERGEANT!"

"Went crying to your friend's buddy to get into dog-training school, did you, Private?"

"I never cry, SERGEANT!"

"You know how many dead men I've seen, Private?"

Rick stopped a second. The guys didn't like to think about that aspect of the war, but the sergeants liked to remind them.

"No, Sergeant," Rick said more quietly.

Sarge spoke quietly as well. "Two hundred and seven. I keep a record."

Rick didn't answer.

"Fifty push-ups, Private, and don't ever yawn in front of me again! If you yawn at the wrong moment in Vietnam, you'll be a dead man. Understand what I'm saying, Private?"

"Yes, SERGEANT!"

Rick dropped to the ground and executed fifty perfect push-ups while the other men left to run their dogs down the road.

Cracker sat patiently, and when Rick was finished, he could swear that dog was laughing at him.

Five

CRACKER LIKED TRAINING A LOT NOW. SHE HAD FUN doing what Rick wanted the second she was sure what it was or sometimes even the second she thought she knew what it was. Back with Willie, she felt like she was the center of the world. She didn't quite feel that with Rick, but she felt she was doing important work, and she liked that.

Cracker's favorite part of her new life was when they all started going out into the field and finding men hiding in bushes, guns buried in holes, and anything that smelled or sounded wrong. Rick taught her what was "wrong," like wind whooshing over a taut string, the smell of gunpowder, growling at the other guys, a hole dug in the ground hidden by leaves, and especially biting certain people. That happened only once, and it wasn't really her fault. The guy had reached out really fast, and she had been surprised. So she didn't see how Rick could blame her for that.

Then sometimes they would spend the night out there, and she would lie in the darkness with images of the day drifting through her head. She would see the food she'd eaten or the hidden man jumping out of the bushes. Other nights she would listen to Rick, Cody, and Twenty-Twenty talk. Every so often as they talked, she would hear "Cracker" in their conversation, so she would listen more closely, but she didn't know what they said.

She always stuck with Rick. She felt the absence of Willie, but it wasn't an anger anymore. She had started to feel happy whenever Rick was around. He would pet her even while he talked to the other men. She liked that.

Rick, too, would often lie quietly under the stars and think of the day, usually of how well Cracker had done and how well he felt the two of them were starting to understand each other. As a matter of fact, he thought *she* was going to whip the world. The previous week on the way to a training session he'd inadvertently made the crawl gesture, and Cracker immediately crouched and looked up at

him, ready to crawl. A number of times she
down when he'd only just placed his tongue on t
of his mouth to pronounce "down." Previously, thi
had bothered him, but she'd gotten the timing so
exact that she didn't do it before he wanted her to
but she still did it before he finished speaking. In
fact, he got the feeling that getting the timing perfect
was one of her favorite things.

Even on the day they practiced flying on a helicopter, she seemed intent on jumping onto the
chopper at the precise moment that he did.

Cracker loved the chopper, how the scents from
the air flooded her and vanished almost simultaneously. Everything Cracker could feel on the outside,
she could also feel on the inside.

The squad was also supposed to practice rap-
pelling that day. That was when you put on a harness and jumped off with your dog. But the chopper
malfunctioned, and they ended up skipping that.

After about six weeks they started what Rick figured was the most important part of training. So far
they'd searched for booby traps and personnel that
the handlers already knew the location of. Finally,
they were going to spend a week bivouacking with
their dogs and searching for booby traps and personnel whose locations were unknown to them.

Before this aspect of training, a bunch of guys planned to take their minuscule paychecks and have themselves a weekend of fun in Atlanta. But Rick didn't get a pass, and Cody and Twenty-Twenty decided to stick around. Rick didn't much like the big city anyway.

Saturday morning the sun warmed the back of Rick's neck as he, Cody, and Twenty-Twenty walked to the kennels together. Cody and Twenty-Twenty had become good buddies of his, though they didn't have a lot in common. Rick was glad to know he'd have a couple of pals in Vietnam. Cody and Rick were from fair-size Midwestern towns, and Twenty-Twenty was from Phoenix. Cody hardly ever worried, while for no particular reason, Twenty-Twenty worried all the time. Rick wasn't much of a worrier either. On those rare occasions back home when he did worry, he just went into the shop in the garage and sanded a table, fixed a chair.

After they took out their dogs, Cody told them about something he'd seen on TV—some variety show he was obsessed with. The whole idea was to get their three dogs to move in unison. "Dancing dogs," Cody called it. It worked great. The dogs learned it in about three minutes. Left paw! Right paw! Heel! Heel! Heel! It seemed like they had half the guys in camp watching. Finally, they got chewed out by a lieutenant colonel for playing with the "well-oiled military equipment"—that is, the dogs. So they put the dogs away and went to mail call.

Rick had heard that when you got to Vietnam, you lived for mail from home. Rick got regular mail from his family, of course. And about once every week Rick had been getting a letter from this Willie kid. Rick wrote to his parents about the training, trying to make it sound as fun as possible, and then told them that they'd be starting an important aspect of training soon. He asked about the family and so forth. Just the usual stuff, yet it felt good. It made you feel like you were still a part of the real world. He didn't write the kid back, though. He only had so much free time. He tried once, but he didn't want the boy to think that he might get Cracker back someday: He wouldn't.

That night after he dropped off his mail, he ate with his buddies in the mess hall, chowing down some pretty decent hamburgers. They weren't like Mom made, but they weren't half bad.

"So does U-Haul have it out for me or what?" Rick said.

Cody laughed, sharing his mouth full of food with the table.

"Aw, man," Rick said. "Close your mouth!" That could get you banned for life at *his* house.

Twenty-Twenty said, "For all intensive purposes, many teachers I've had in life seemed to like some students more than others and some students less than others. But sometimes—and again, for all intensive purposes—the students they seemed to like less were occasionally their favorites underneath it all. It happened once in a herpetology course I took."

"Herpetology?" Rick said. "That sounds like some kind of disease."

"It's the study of reptiles and amphibians."

"Studying that crud oughta be illegal," Rick said. "You gonna finish those fries?"

"I already got dibs," said Cody.

"Since when?"

"I asked him yesterday, because I heard we were having burgers today." Cody grinned. A line of ketchup squiggled down the front of his shirt.

Twenty-Twenty, who was meticulous about his person, said, "You got ketchup all over your outfit!"

"Outfit!" Cody and Rick cried out in unison. "Did you say *outfit*?"

Cody added, "My *sister* wears outfits."

A guy from another table yelled out, "It's 'uniform,' or 'fatigues,' or somethin', but one thing I know is, I ain't wearing no *outfit*." They all howled while Twenty-Twenty wore his usual serious expression.

When they finished eating, it was still warm out. Sometimes after dinner Rick, Twenty-Twenty, and Cody caught a jeep toward the kennels. For the return trip they caught a delivery truck.

Today Rick, Cody, and Twenty-Twenty decided to catch a late jeep. The sky was growing dim, and the sun slanted into Rick's eyes. "Hey, your mom still want to get that beeshon freeze?" Rick said.

Twenty-Twenty said, "It's pronounced bichon frise. It costs three hundred dollars. Where is my dad going to get three hundred dollars? But she says it looks like a cloud."

Rick laughed. "Three hundred dollars for a cloud?"

Cracker, Bruno, and Tristie sat patiently at their individual kennel gates, but when they saw their guys, the impatience turned to near hysteria. As soon as the gates opened, Cracker and Tristie tore across a field, Tristie nipping at Cracker's back legs. Finally, they circled back to see their guys. Bruno just watched in his stately manner.

Rick, Cody, and Twenty-Twenty sauntered across a field with the dogs. Tonight for some reason, grasshoppers or something were jumping all over the place. Rick swatted one away while the dogs—even Bruno—went after them.

Cracker jumped up and grabbed one in her mouth. *Yuck.* She let it drop out. Then she went to sit next to Rick, resting her head on one of his legs.

"I heard they eat grasshoppers in Vietnam," Cody said. "Ever try it?"

Rick and Twenty-Twenty looked at each other. "Ever try *what*?" Rick finally said.

"Eating a grasshopper," Cody said, as if it were obvious.

Twenty-Twenty flapped his hands with exasperation. "Just because they eat them in Vietnam, *if* they eat them in Vietnam, doesn't mean you have to try it. That's why we live in America, so we don't have to eat crap like that."

Cody shrugged. "That's not why I live in America. I was born here."

Rick laughed. "I don't know if they eat grasshoppers or not, but I do know that I ain't trying one." He lay back on his elbows and lit a cigarette. Twenty-Twenty and Cody were great friends, but they fought like an old married couple. He flashed on a memory of his maternal grandfather shortly before he died. They used to keep chickens in the barn for dinner. You killed them by grabbing their heads and shaking them in a circle. One night when his grandpa was getting really old, he went out to get the night's chicken. When he took a long time, Rick's mother sent Rick out to check on him. And there was Grandpa, shaking the chicken in a circle by his feet while Grandma screamed at him. Rick, who was only seven, tried to calm everybody down. Grandpa and Grandma bickered and screamed a lot at the end. The poor chicken was the only calm thing in the barn.

Twenty-Twenty couldn't stop. "I mean, the reason America is America is not that we don't eat grasshoppers."

"You're so literal, man," Cody said innocently.

"Literal? It's human language, it's words, you have to say what you mean. That's what words are for!"

Rick laughed again. "I'm glad I'm not either of you, 'cause you're both nuts." He watched the dogs leap through the air for the grasshoppers. The dogs looked like grasshoppers themselves. He never realized what springy legs dogs had. That is, he'd realized it, but he'd never looked at dogs as closely before as he did every day now. In the backyard of somebody's house they didn't seem like anything but friendly, furry things, but out in nature they were pretty darn impressive. The delivery truck honked, and Rick jumped up. "Cracker. Come!" He and his friends put the dogs away and hopped on the truck.

Monday morning was hot as a summer day. But U-Haul seemed to think the weather was some kind of gift from the heavens. "Perfect training weather for Vietnam, men!" The platoon was trucked over to the kennels slightly later than usual, so most of the dogs were already sitting at the front gate waiting. Rick looked down the row of men and dogs and saw the faces of both light up as they saw each other. Many of the dogs jumped up and down. Cracker barked a couple of times as if to reprimand Rick for being a few minutes late.

"Sorry," Rick told her.

She pawed the gate. She forgave him.

Six

As Rick headed for formation, adrenaline pumped through him. He, Twenty-Twenty, and Cody were now in an unspoken race to be the best in the class. Like last week, when Cracker had not only sniffed out the booby trap she was supposed to, but the sergeant had let her go for an entire hour, finding trap after trap and a couple of hidden men. She even sniffed out a man hiding underwater. She was a thing of wonder, and so far she was the only dog to sniff out a man underwater. Rick figured all he'd get for his troubles would be a stripe for a promotion, a minuscule pay raise, and a cheap trophy. But fair was fair: They were becoming the best dog team, and he knew it. Cody and Twenty-Twenty probably thought they were the best teams, and while Rick had to admit Bruno and Tristie were pretty good, well, he just thought Cracker was better. It was nothing personal against the other dogs.

But there was another reason Rick wanted to be best: He planned to come home without getting hurt. Rick had read the training manual twice, and he'd never read a book twice in his life. He planned to read the manual one more time before training ended. He wanted everything to be second nature by the time he got to Vietnam. That way, he had a better chance of DEROSing in one piece. DEROS meant "date of expected return from overseas."

Another guy passed with his dog, and Rick kind of looked away. The guy knew he'd pulled a bad dog, a scrawny mutt with the ridiculous moniker of Adonis. Adonis just didn't seem to have the knack. He hit booby traps with such regularity that the guys called him "No Nose." Rick had to admit that he now felt secretly thankful to U-Haul for assigning him to Cracker.

Rick slowed down when he heard Cody call out behind him. "Rick, you think they're feeding the dogs enough?" Cody said. "Bruno's always hungry."

"I dunno," Rick said. He lowered his voice. "I give Cracker treats every so often."

Cody lowered his voice. "Sometimes I give Bruno an extra meal."

Cracker suddenly lunged at something. Rick pulled hard on her leash. "No!"

Twenty-Twenty leaned over. "It's a snake." He leaned closer. "It's an Eastern hognose!"

Rick struggled to control Cracker. "Sit!" he shouted, and finally she did. He shook her snout. "Bad girl!" He sure didn't want her going after snakes or other animals in Vietnam.

The handlers and their dogs fell into formation as U-Haul approached carrying a chicken, of all things. Twenty-four men stood together in the platoon. The guys all glanced at one another as if U-Haul was crazy, which of course he was. The sergeant started to shout but halted as several helicopters roared overhead. Nearly all of the dogs strained on their leashes to reach the chicken. Cracker was going wild.

A private Rick had never seen joined Sarge as the helicopters continued to roar. The way Rick heard it, the Vietnam War was sometimes called the "Helicopter War." With choppers, entire companies could maneuver with greater speed than ever before. Each chopper would carry ten or so men at a time for a big battle and later fly the soldiers back to base camp for a warm meal that night in the mess hall. At least, that's the way Rick pictured it.

Even before the helicopters had completely passed, the sergeant was already screaming, though not *at* anyone. He just paced back and forth screaming. Rumor was Sarge screamed in his sleep. "You cannot stop a dog from alerting at an animal. But you must control your dog. Your dog must understand that it is not his job to hunt down animals."

The chicken squawked nervously. The dogs barked wildly, pulling hard on their leashes. Except Bruno. Bruno was mighty interested in the chicken, but he sat under control at Cody's side. Meanwhile, it took all Rick's strength to control Cracker. Finally, he shouted, "NO!" and gave a hard jerk on the chain, and she sulkily sat down. Drool began puddling beneath her on the ground. *Damn,* he thought. He'd seen dogs like her before, where the prey drive ran like wolf blood through them. One farmer he remembered had ended up shooting his own dog when she killed half his chickens. Then Cracker tried a new tactic, sitting her best sit in front of him. "No!" he cried.

After a moment Sarge handed the terrified chicken to the private next to him. "Okay, you can take her back to the chef," he said. He turned to the squad. "Got a senator visiting Benning for dinner tonight. Need to have some kind of special gourmet chicken."

The private walked off with the senator's dinner.

Sarge looked at the men suddenly and shouted, "The scout dog must be trained to work on airborne scent alone!" Rick mouthed the words with him: He knew that part by heart; they all did.

Sarge bellowed, "These are scout dogs, not trackers. A dog with his nose on the ground tracking a ground scent might lead you directly into ambush. Determine wind and terrain upon arrival to the mission site. Think. THINK. Think about the scent cone. Private Lanski, what does a strong wind mean?" U-Haul always said Rick's name wrong. Always. But annoying as it was, Rick wasn't about to correct him because he figured that's exactly what U-Haul was trying to goad him into doing.

Instead, he shouted back, "Sergeant! A strong wind means a narrow scent cone!" The scent cone was the three-dimensional shape a scent made in the air. The center of the cone was the booby trap, weapons cache, food cache, Vietcong soldier, or whatever else the dog was smelling. Given even terrain and stable wind conditions, scent moved outward from the center in the shape of a cone. If you didn't watch your dog carefully, you could lead him right out of the scent cone.

The men waited while U-Haul stood speechless. Rick moved his eyes but couldn't see what U-Haul was staring at. Then a general's daughter walked by. She was cute as hell, but a snotty little princess. She liked to walk by the enlisted men and ignore them.

"Never take your eyes off your dog," Sarge resumed shouting, directly at Rick. "If there is one rule you must always follow in the field, it's never take your eyes off your dog. Your slack man will protect your back." A "slack man" was the bodyguard who was assigned to each dog-handling team. A team was one man, one dog: inseparable. The handler watched the dog, and the slack man guarded the handler. Rick tried not to look bored. Cracker panted eagerly. Finally, Sarge stopped shouting.

Cracker was looking adoringly at Rick. He smiled at her.

"Private, are you listening!"

Rick looked up. "Absolutely, Sergeant! You said—"

"I said, in this part of the training your dog is no longer simply following your orders. You are following your dog. If your dog alerts, you must be watching. Always. You become a single entity. Never take your eyes off your dog. They got as many beautiful girls in Vietnam as any country in the universe. They got nothing but girls. They got more beautiful girls than leaves in the jungle."

One of the guys said, "Woo-hoo!"

Now, if Rick had said "woo-hoo," he'd be doing push-ups until lunchtime, but U-Haul ignored the other guy. Still, Rick called out, "Yes, Sergeant! Leaves in the jungle, SERGEANT!" Tact and diplomacy! His parents had taught him fairness; now he was learning politics.

The men loaded their gear, including tents, onto the trucks that would take them to field training. They were crossing the border into Alabama today. A couple of guys had to tie up their more aggressive dogs before helping load. One of the guys had a dog who was just plain crazy. The dog wouldn't let anyone within ten feet of his handler, and he howled for hours when he and his handler were separated. But he seemed to have good sniffing abilities, so the army was holding on to him.

Cracker didn't think the dog was crazy. He was just protecting his handler. She kind of respected him. She yawned and lay patiently next to Bruno and Tristie as Rick, Cody, and Twenty-Twenty worked. Whenever the guys loaded the truck, it meant they were going away for a while to sleep in the field. She liked that. The loud man started shouting so loudly that Cracker moved her eyes away from Rick. "Remember, in the field you never take your eyes off the dog." Cracker moved her eyes back to Rick and felt a slight thrill as he moved his eyes to *her*. A soft drizzle fell on her nose. She could smell the loud man from where she lay. He smelled loud, just like Cody smelled happy, Rick smelled calm and confident, and Twenty-Twenty smelled worried. Rick looked away. Cracker rested her nose on Tristie's back.

When the truck was loaded, Rick looked at Cracker and called out, "Hup!" Cracker timed her leap onto the truck to coincide with when Rick hopped up. She landed a second before he did and turned to wait for him. "Good girl," he said. She wagged her tail. The sarge came near her, and she growled. Rick grabbed her leash. "No!" he said, and she sat down. She liked the same people and dogs Rick liked. He obviously didn't like the sarge.

The truck rumbled through the rain. The rain destroyed some of the smells that Cracker was used to, but it also created new, wet smells. Once, the truck passed a deer along the highway, and all the dogs hung off the side barking furiously. Cracker thought about jumping off, but she had a feeling

Rick wouldn't like that. If it were Willie, she would have done it anyway and let him come get her. She hadn't thought of Willie for a while. He'd been her best friend. But she and Rick had something else, something bigger. She wasn't sure what it was. All she knew was that when he came to her in the morning, she had no choice but to twirl around and chase her tail before sitting down in front of him. She'd always celebrated when Willie came home too, but this was different. With Willie, she'd felt that when they were separated, he was where he was, and she was where she was. But with Rick, she felt she was kind of with him all the time; and when he came in person, she was even more with him.

As soon as the truck stopped and everybody jumped off, Cracker gave herself a good shake. All the other dogs gave themselves a good shake. All the men held up their hands and called out, "No!" Cracker thought that was funny.

The rain stopped and the air grew heavy with scents. Cracker lifted her nose and sniffed. A feeling of joy washed through her. So many good smells!

"What direction is the wind blowing, Private?" cried out the loud man.

Rick saw that Cracker's nose had lifted toward the northwest. "From the northwest, Sergeant."

"Think you're smart, Private?"

"I'm sorry, Sergeant?"

"I said, think you're smart, Private?"

"No, SERGEANT!"

"Think you're dumb, Private?"

"No, SERGEANT!"

"Well, which is it, smart or dumb?"

Rick hesitated before realizing there was no right answer. So he said, "Cracker and I are going to whip the world, SERGEANT!"

Rick could tell that the sergeant liked his answer. Sarge turned suddenly toward Cody. "What the hell are you grinning about?"

"Nothing, Sergeant!" cried out Cody.

Sarge snapped back to Rick. "Go to it, soldier."

Rick performed the crossover, removing Cracker's choke chain and slipping on her work harness. That's how she knew life was about to get serious.

Rick secured anything on Cracker or himself that might jingle and alert the enemy. He taped his dog tags together as they'd been taught to do. He wanted to ask whether they weren't going to set up camp first, but Sarge was looking at him impatiently. So he said quietly but urgently, "Search, Cracker. Search!"

She surged forward. Rick jerked the leash to correct her. Not too fast, or she might miss something. In Vietnam that could cost Rick his life.

Cracker loved running. She loved pulling, too. Rick didn't like when she pulled, but she didn't hold that against him. She restrained herself as she moved forward into a shallow swamp, Rick following. The other men lagged far behind. The mud-colored swamp sucked at her feet with each step, making a soft *shlurp* noise as she moved her paws. But she smelled something important. She stood very still, her ears rotating in the direction of the sound, her nose raised to sniff. There it was! She pointed her nose, then turned with pride to Rick. A bird in a tree!

He jerked at her leash. The sarge had told them that you could never, ever teach a dog not to alert to animals. But you had to discourage it anyway. He thought again of the farmer who'd shot his dog, but he pushed the thought out of his mind.

"No! Search!" Rick said.

Rick felt annoyed. Cracker had improved since he'd met her, but every so often she surprised him by taking off after a squirrel or a bird. Rick rearranged the rucksack on his back. It weighed fifty-five pounds, less than he would carry most days in Nam, but it already felt heavy. Swamp water and sweat drenched his clothes. Sweat dripped into his eyes. He already wanted to take off his steel pot—or helmet—but if he did, a piece of shrapnel might hit him. Of course, since this was just training, there was no shrapnel. But Rick resisted the urge to take off his helmet. He needed to get used to it, and he knew U-Haul would yell at him if he took it off.

Cracker gazed longingly at the bird again but felt the chain jerk on her neck. She'd killed a bird once while she and Willie were out in a forest. She knew it was a "bird" because Willie had taught her that word. She would never forget killing the bird because it was so much fun. But she could feel Rick's annoyance. She sniffed at the air. There was something . . . a smell Rick had taught her about. The scent seemed stronger to the left.

Cracker waded through the swamp, thinking of only one thing now: the smell to the left. She pulled Rick out of the swamp and walked directly into the smell. It was everywhere, flooding into her nose. And she heard the faint, whistling rhythm of someone breathing. She pricked up her ears. She could also smell the breath coming from whomever was breathing.

"Whatcha got, girl?" Rick said urgently.

She felt the hair on her back stand up. "Grrrr," she answered him. *Ouch!* Rick had yanked the harness.

"Quiet," he whispered.

She charged suddenly, and a man jumped from a thick bush and ran off. She lunged after him, ripping at his pants. Rick called, "Stay! Stay!" Cracker reluctantly stopped.

"Good girl!" Rick said. Cracker felt his face rubbing all over hers. "Good girl!" he said again. She rubbed her face back against his. She felt satisfied all over.

Then she lifted her head sharply. She still heard something. She turned back to where the man had run from and stood straight up. From far away, she heard a sound Rick had taught her to listen for: the sound of wind passing around a wire pulled tight. She faintly smelled gunpowder.

She looked up at Rick, questioning him, and he looked at the loud man, who nodded. Rick said, "Search, girl."

She knew exactly where the sound was coming from, so she pulled Rick more than she knew he liked. But she didn't pull so much that he reprimanded her. She was getting to know him really well. The forest grew denser, the smell dispersed, but the sound was unmistakable. As soon as she was sure what it was, and where, she sat down and stared toward the source of the sound.

Rick said, "Whatcha got, girl?"

She looked at him, then turned back to the sound. Couldn't he hear it?

Rick repeated, "What you got, girl?"

He stepped around her and cautiously moved forward, scanning up and down to make sure he didn't miss anything. Cracker followed him and pawed him once.

Rick knew he'd tripped the wire almost before he actually tripped it. Later he wondered *how* he'd known beforehand. Unfortunately, he didn't know in time to stop. The booby trap exploded, though of course it wasn't real gunpowder. Rick wanted to kick himself. And it was all his fault. Cracker had given a strong alert, and he'd moved past her because he hadn't seen anything.

The instructor moved up beside him. "You know what the soldiers fighting in Vietnam would call that, Private?"

"I don't know, Sergeant."

"A BK," the instructor said.

During three months of basic, three months of AIT, and now dog-handling school, Rick had learned a lot of the slang that the guys used in Vietnam. It was supposedly like a whole new language. But he hadn't heard "BK" yet. "What's a BK?" he asked dejectedly.

"That stands for 'below-the-knee amputation.'" The instructor turned to the rest of the squad. "All right, who's up next?"

The next team moved forward. Rick, Cracker, and the others lagged about sixty yards behind so as not to interfere with whatever the point dog was smelling. "Point" meant in front. One of the dog teams' primary jobs in country would be to walk point in front of all the other soldiers. This was one of the most dangerous jobs in Vietnam, because it meant that if there was a booby trap, you would come upon it first.

Rick's dejection turned his legs to lead. He'd let Cracker down and he'd let himself down. Cracker sniffed at him, as if trying to smell his feelings. "Good girl," he whispered, and she felt happy because he said that, but also kind of sad because she could tell he felt sad.

Seven

THE REST OF THE DAY DRAGGED. ONE BY ONE THE other teams took their turns at point. Only Cody and Bruno performed perfectly. Rick had hoped to get another turn, but the squad barely had time to get through everybody. And he was exhausted anyway.

After eight hours of humping the fields, the men settled in a grassy area as far away as possible from the swamps. Still, Cracker could smell the swampland everywhere. At first she'd liked the smell of decaying leaves, but now her nose felt full of it. She could hear mosquitoes buzzing everywhere. Every so often one of the men would clap at the air and cry out in triumph.

"Get used to mosquitoes," said the sarge. "You're going to meet a lot of them in your future."

Rick took out the army-issue insect repellent that the men kept under a strap around their helmets.

"What're you doing, soldier?" said the sarge.

Now what?

The sarge said, "We're in enemy territory. No bug juice."

"But, Sarge . . . ," said Rick. He felt that righteous indignation rise inside himself.

"Charlie can smell it. Charlie can smell almost as good as your dog. Charlie is quieter than a cat. Charlie is more audacious than a monkey. Charlie will smell that bug juice in half a second if you use it."

Rick wondered vaguely what "audacious" meant. "Charlie" was what soldiers in country called the Vietcong. It was short for "Victor Charles." In the army every letter of the alphabet had a word assigned to it, so radio operators could make sure no mistakes were made while they talked to one another. "A" was "alpha," "B" was "bravo," "C" was "Charles," or "Charlie," and so on.

"Then what's the point of giving it to us?" Rick asked.

"Are you mouthing off, soldier?"

Rick could see that U-Haul was about to

explode. "No, Sergeant, I'm trying to learn," Rick said. "I appreciate your superior knowledge on all matters, Sergeant." *Tact and diplomacy, dammit.*

"That's the right attitude, mister. Malaria's a problem over there. For the information of you know-nothings, malaria is carried by mosquitoes. You can use bug juice around camp but not out in the forward areas."

Rick wanted to ask, *Why wear us down before we even get to Vietnam?* He considered sneaking bug juice on his face. But if he got caught, he might even get written up again. He squished a mosquito on his arm, saw the blood gush out of it.

He tried not to think about it. Instead, he stuck his fingers into Cracker's coat and felt her for ticks. Then he ran his fingers backward through her hair, then forward. Then he brushed her hair. Cracker had already shed her inner coat. German shepherds had two coats, but the inner one, which was mostly down, shed every summer or in hot weather. Cracker's eyes shone as Rick brushed her.

She relaxed as his fingers moved back and forth. *Good Rick. Good boy.* When Rick tried to stop brushing her, she pawed him for more. She liked his sweaty smell. She liked the way he brushed her. She liked the food he gave her. She liked being outside.

She pushed up close to him. She liked being outside near his smell with him brushing her.

Tristie walked over to sniff at her. They touched noses, and then Tristie returned to Twenty-Twenty.

As he brushed Cracker, Rick calculated. Several of the handlers had made multiple mistakes today. He'd made only one—not that he cared about a trophy or anything. He figured the time would come when even Bruno and Cody would make a mistake while Rick and Cracker would not. He lit a cigarette from the one he was already smoking. For some reason, he always savored the first drag of a cigarette the most. Theoretically, if you couldn't use bug juice, you couldn't smoke a cigarette, but since U-Haul chain-smoked a combination of cigars and cigarettes, that rule went down the drain.

The men began opening their C rations. Rick blew smoke into the air as he listened to some guys talk about the Atlanta Braves and the Falcons. He saw Cody eyeing everybody's C rats, probably thinking up deals to strike. Rick had pulled ham 'n' chokers, which everybody except Cody agreed was the worst C rat available. The "chokers" were lima beans—that is, the nastiest vegetable Mother Nature had ever invented. Cody said, "Trade you for my meatballs?"

Rick jumped at it. "Deal!" Spaghetti and meatballs was considered one of the primest of the prime
C rations. Even with just the meatballs, Rick felt like
he'd struck gold.

Rick took out the empty can that they all carried
as a stove to heat their meals. You placed Trioxin
heat tabs inside and poked holes in the bottom to
keep fumes from building up inside the can. The
army issued these heat tabs, but supposedly, soldiers in country used C-4 explosive to heat their
food. C-4 exploded only with heat *and* impact. A
match caused the C-4 to heat up like the devil himself was cooking your food. Rick and some guys had
tried it once during advanced infantry training. It
was like putty, and you shaped it into a ball the size
of a quarter, with a little point on top. Cooked your
C rats in thirty seconds flat. Heated your coffee
instantaneously.

Sarge was enjoying a cigar, alternately puffing
on it and smiling at it. Cody leaned toward Rick.
"U-Haul almost wigged big-time when you ques-
tioned him about the bug juice. You better lie low."

"Yeah," Rick said softly. "Thanks."

Rick took out the P-38 can opener he'd attached
to his dog-tag chain to open C rations. Cody was
saying to someone, "I'll trade you four ciggies for

your fruit salad." Cody was the only man in the squad who didn't smoke.

Rick opened Cracker's food first. He dumped it into his steel pot the way Sarge had told them to do. She gobbled the food, and then he poured in water from one of her canteens. Cracker waited for more food.

Rick said, "No, girl. We travel light in the field. One meal a day." She whimpered but lapped up some water before laying her head down, eyes turned sadly toward Rick. *Aw, for crying out loud.*

"Hey, Sarge?" Rick wheedled. "Cracker's twice as big as some of the dogs. Shouldn't she get more food?"

"One can per dog in the field," the sergeant said. "How many times do I have to tell you guys?"

Rick and Twenty-Twenty met eyes, and Twenty-Twenty slipped a bit of Tristie's food to Cracker. Cracker swallowed it and felt it slide unchewed down her throat. She laid her paw over Rick's ankle as he ate his own dinner, but just because she liked her paw there, not to ask him for anything. She never begged him while he was eating. He hated that more than anything. Willie had always handed her treats while he ate. Willie had always done whatever she wanted. A brief anxiety washed over her at the thought of Willie. But life was good here, too.

The sun sank over the forest as the men ate and smoked. One of the guys who apparently thought he was going to kiss butt to a promotion squatted down near U-Haul. "We're lucky to have your wisdom and experience, Sergeant. So what's it like in Nam?" the guy asked.

Sarge belched and cleared his throat before speaking. "Wetter than anything you've ever experienced," he said. "Or so dry your tongue feels like paper, depending on the season. And hot, no matter what the season. When it rains, it rains for weeks. We had one guy drown on a hilltop that flooded during a monsoon rain. None of the birds could get to him because of the weather." "Birds" were helicopters. "They found his body later on top of a dry hill. The doc said he'd drowned."

Rick contemplated that. Personally, he would have abandoned his gear and swam to safety.

"Why didn't he swim?" someone asked.

"To where?" the sarge asked simply. "The whole countryside was flooded. And the guy was star of his swim team in high school."

Rick contemplated *that*.

"Does the enemy use dogs?" another soldier asked.

"Nah, but they put a bounty on both our dogs and our handlers. The rumor is that they pay anywhere from one thousand to twenty thousand U.S. dollars to anyone who brings them a dog's tattooed ear."

Rick wondered whether that was true. One thousand or twenty, it was a lot of money for a dog's ear.

Rick lay on his back in the grass. Cracker stretched on her back and kicked her legs in the air. The shadows had grown long. The forest was peaceful.

Twenty-Twenty was rolling his eyes around. One thing Rick had learned was that every man had a quirk, just as every dog did. Twenty-Twenty did weird eye exercises, Cody was always grinning, Jonesie walked in his sleep, and Petrocelli said "um" every other word. Rick didn't know what his own quirk was. His righteous indignation? That wasn't a quirk. Maybe generalists didn't have quirks. "For all intensive purposes, I'm getting sleepy," Twenty-Twenty said.

Twenty-Twenty continued moving his eyes around and up and down, which he did every night. He claimed it was some kind of ancient Chinese method of keeping your eyes strong, but he looked like a nutcase. Rick called out, "Hey, man, you look like a nutcase!"

Twenty-Twenty looked at him seriously. "For all intensive purposes, this is the best way to keep your eyes strong."

That was too much for Cody, who started laughing. "That doesn't even make sense!" he said.

Twenty-Twenty just wrinkled his brow. Rick chuckled. But Twenty-Twenty just lay back, took off his glasses, and laid his palms over his eyes to meditate or something. Tristie lay with her head on his stomach. Rick saw several of the dogs like that, and before long Cracker came over and set her head on his own belly.

Rick lit the last of the four cigarettes that had come with his C rations. The moon was full. Under the moonlight Cody was winding his watch. It was a special gold watch his grandfather had given him. Rick didn't own anything of value, but if he had, he certainly wouldn't have brought it here. But Cody had been close to his grandfather and loved his watch.

Rick tried to imagine a man drowning on a hilltop alone underneath the same peaceful moon now lighting up the sky. He could picture the whole scenario, but only as a movie. He couldn't imagine it really happening. "Hey, Sarge?" he said. "That really a true story about the guy drowning on a hilltop?"

U-Haul just laughed at him. "You got a lot to learn about whipping the world, Lanski. A whole lot."

Eight

ONCE IT GOT FUN, TRAINING PASSED QUICKLY.
One rainy day during formation, Cracker could feel
uncertainty in the air. Her paws sank into the mud.
Usually, Rick didn't make her stand out in such hard
rain for so long. She kept looking up at him waiting
for him to take her away, but he didn't move. He
seemed funny today, not sad exactly and not scared.
More like uncertain, like he didn't know what was
going to happen next. And he always knew what was
going to happen. What happened tomorrow was just
about exactly the same thing that had happened the
day before. So what was there to be uncertain
about? She looked up at him again. She was so wet,
it was hard to see.

It was the last day of class, and the twenty-four

men of the 67th Infantry Platoon (Scout Dog) stood at attention with their dogs. Rain poured. Rick saw Sarge holding a couple of cheap trophies in his hands and felt a twinge of pride and anticipation. The last weeks of training had gone perfectly, as far as Rick was concerned. He and Cracker had not made a single error.

"This rain is nothing," said the sergeant to the men. "Get used to it." He said "This is nothing" whenever any hardship occurred. He held up the trophies, which were about the size of cans of beer. "Willis, trophy for first place. Butler, second." Cody and Twenty-Twenty stepped forward to get their trophies as Rick felt his face grow hot. U-Haul looked at him. "Not a bad job . . . , Hanski." So that was going to be Rick's only trophy: getting his name pronounced correctly, for once.

U-Haul didn't talk long. The rain drenched his face and clothes as he addressed the platoon. Rick had never seen him so sober. The most memorable line of the day was some graffiti U-Haul quoted: "Join the army, meet interesting people, then kill 'em." He said, "That's what it all comes down to, men. See you in a month."

What did a trophy mean? Rick could've made one in his dad's tool shop that looked twice as good as the ones Cody and Twenty-Twenty got. But he felt his confidence wane—he'd really wanted one of those trophies. His confidence returned as he packed his bag for home leave and thought of Cracker the whole time. His new closeness to Cracker made him feel that it was still possible to whip the world. It was just that maybe doing so was going to be a lot harder than he'd thought. How much harder was the important issue. He looked up and saw Cody standing beside him.

"We're gonna make it back safe," Cody said. "You got a great dog."

"Get out of my head, you mind-readin' freak."

Cody laughed. "You don't need to be a freak to read your simple mind." Then he added seriously, "We're gonna make it, I know it."

Cody really was the most optimistic guy in the world. Rick pushed himself up and stuck out his hand. The two men shook. Cody started to walk away, and Rick called out, "Cody!"

Cody turned around. "Yeah?"

"I'll be watching your back in Nam."

Cody grinned. "Likewise."

Rick went out in the rain, fell to his knees, and did something he rarely did: He prayed. He prayed that all twenty-four soldiers of the 67th IPSD would

95

be DEROSed in one piece. He prayed for the guys who, through bad luck, had been teamed up with so-so dogs. Of course, not long ago he'd thought he was one of those guys. He heard whooping and turned around to see Cody and Twenty-Twenty descending on him.

"You think praying is gonna save you from Vietnam?" shouted Cody.

Cody and Twenty-Twenty picked up Rick and threw him into the mud. Rick picked Cody up and threw *him* into the mud. "I don't need no trophy to tell me Cracker and I are gonna be the best dog team in Vietnam!" Rick cried out.

"In your dreams!" Cody cried back. "Dream on!"

Nine

THE NEXT DAY RICK HUGGED CRACKER SO HARD, it scared her. It was sudden, the hugging. At first he'd just petted her, given her a wiener. She remembered Willie's last hug. She whined.

"Don't worry," he said. "It's just a leave before we get sent to Vietnam. They'll take good care of you, I promise. If they don't, I'll kill 'em."

Then the next day he didn't show up at all. She tried not to get too upset—it was just one day—and someone came to feed her and water her. But she got the sense that Rick was far away. She stuck her nose against the fence, and Tristie pushed her nose against hers. Tristie was worried too. None of the guys had come by today.

She couldn't imagine that Rick had left her. But

yesterday there had been a lot of anxiety with the guys, and with the dogs. Something was up, but what? Why all the hugging? One guy even cried. Rick had said, "Last wiener for a while." She knew "wiener," of course, but what did the rest mean?

Then all week, whining up and down the row. She and Tristie slept next to each other, pushed together against the chain link on their wooden platforms. Week after week. Another guy would walk her, but he walked some of the other dogs, too. He wasn't her guy. One night she emitted a high hum that she'd never heard from herself before. Not a whine exactly, and not a cry. Just a high, sad hum. Tristie joined her, and pretty soon the whole row of dogs followed. A couple of humans even stopped by to listen. One said, "Did you ever hear anything like that before?"

The other replied, "That's the life of a dog, man. You need your human."

Rick's house was old but real nice. Big yard. Big rooms. He spent most of his time in the shop in the garage, making a doghouse, actually, for a family down the street. He'd never made a doghouse before. He'd always figured dogs could sleep anywhere. But now he not only built the house but attached a plywood porch, with a roof for the dog to lie under during the summer.

His bedroom hadn't changed a bit, but he didn't feel at home there. It was like something was missing. He found himself lying in bed thinking about Cracker. Man, he was getting weird. He wondered how much weirder he might get in Vietnam. He'd heard that some of the guys who went there—not just the handlers—got old fast.

Even his mother made some remark at breakfast: "You've changed."

"What do you mean, I've changed?"

"You've lost weight," his father said, forking at a pancake.

"I'm in the army, man."

"And you're ruder," snapped his grandmother.

Rick didn't answer. He never talked back to his grandparents.

Manning, Wisconsin. Solid, middle-class town. Hardworking people. Good manners. Lot of Scandinavian blood in his area. But he already felt like he didn't fit in with the guys his age around him. They seemed like kids, hanging out at fast-food restaurants, talking about school and girls. A year ago he had been a kid. His grandparents acted like he still was a kid.

Before he left, he cleaned his room real well. He wanted everything in order for . . . whatever. There was another party for him, some of the old-timers playing saws like violins again. As he watched his parents dance to a slow song and the old men playing their saws and his school friends talking, he already felt separated from everyone. Then someone put on a fast record, and he had to laugh at the sight of his parents trying to dance like his friends. Pretty embarrassing. After the party, his father watched the late news. Vietnam this and Vietnam that. He helped around the house and the store—took out garbage, stocked T squares and metal cutters, the usual—but it was just playacting. The real stuff—that was coming. That was coming.

Ten

He was back! But Cracker was mooning so badly that she didn't know it until she saw Tristie hopping around her kennel. And then she felt it. He was back! When he opened the cage, she jumped on him so hard, she knocked him over. "Ow!" he said. "Bad dog!" But then he held her to him.

The twenty-four handlers and their dogs, plus a few extra dogs, separated into three C-130 cargo planes for the trip to Southeast Asia. One soldier drove a deuce-and-a-half—the nickname for a two-and-one-half-ton truck—right onto the plane's ramp. Someone else drove a jeep onto another plane. The men loaded tents, a 105-mm howitzer, M-16 rifles, ammunition, C rations, and everything else they would need to be battle ready the moment they landed in Vietnam. All they lacked, Rick realized, was real-life experience.

Cracker kept turning around in her crate for a glimpse at Rick. She saw men scurrying back and forth carrying boxes and packages. Crates of other dogs surrounded her. Every time Cracker glimpsed Rick, she wagged her tail, but he didn't seem to notice her. Even when he disappeared from sight sometimes, she could often hear and smell him. But she liked to keep him in her sight and strained in her crate for glimpses. She didn't see why she had to wait in here. Finally, Rick and another man carried her in her crate up the ramp and into a big, dark room. Rick knelt next to her and murmured, "Good girl" over and over. "We're going for a ride. Good girl." She knew "ride." And she didn't think he'd leave her like Willie had. She trusted Rick now. She knew he would always come back. She felt sure of it. And she could just see him, sitting on the floor leaning against a wall of the plane.

The rumbling grew so intense, she could hardly hear anything else. Some of the other dogs barked and whined, and one howled hysterically. Then she felt the air pressure change. She felt like she was rising and rising, and yet she didn't seem to be going anywhere. It was different from the ride away from

Willie, and she knew Rick was nearby. But she didn't know what was going on. She could see Bruno in his crate, and she could smell Tristie in hers. Bruno was pressing his nose against his gate. They eyed each other. He wagged his tail; she wagged hers.

Then for a long time there was nothing to do except sleep and pee.

Every so often Cracker would wake up, and nothing would have changed. The room was starting to smell like urine and other things. She sniffed but couldn't smell Rick in the still air. After a long while the plane shook and the air pressure began to change again. Rick came back and put his nose against the gate of her crate. She pushed her nose against his. She sniffed. He smelled good.

"Good girl," he said. "Wet nose!" Then he went away again.

A few times the plane stopped, once someplace really cold and twice someplace really warm. Each time, Rick cleaned out her crate, and then she got back in and the plane took off again, and it was back to the rumbling, to the dim light, to the funny air pressure.

Much later she could feel something different happening in the room, some excitement among the men. Rick came to kneel by her crate and said urgently, "Tonsonoo. Tonsonoo." She wagged her tail. *Tonsonoo!*

Eleven

TAN SON NHUT WAS THE SPRAWLING AIRPORT IN Saigon. Rick crowded at one of the two small windows up front, trying to see over some other men. Down below he just caught sight of jungles, rice paddies, hills, and, in some places, neatly planted rows of trees. Sarge, right at the next window, stabbed at the windowpane. "French-owned rubber-tree plantation," he was saying. "The French colonized Vietnam before World War II, but the Vietnamese kicked their butts in 1954."

As Rick understood it, Vietnam had been one long, narrow country. In 1954 the Geneva Accords divided it into two countries: North Vietnam and South Vietnam. The North Vietnamese were Communist; the South Vietnamese were not. The goal of the United States in this war was to prevent South Vietnam from going Communist. One of the soldiers' goals was to make contact with as many enemy soldiers as possible and kill them. In the army "contact" meant "contact with the enemy," as in firing at or being fired at by the enemy.

The 67th IPSD would be convoying to their final base camp in Bien Hoa, located in what was called "Three Corps." The United States was conducting an air war in North Vietnam, but the ground fighting was only in South Vietnam. The United States had divided South Vietnam into four military regions. Three Corps was second from the bottom.

Rick looked around to see what the other men were doing. Most were pushing at the few windows, but Cody sat in the deuce-and-a-half, sleeping. Unbelievable. Rick couldn't hear him but knew he was snoring. Cody sometimes snored so loudly that the sergeant had decided he might be dangerous during nights spent in hot zones in Vietnam. "Hot zones" were areas where the enemy was active. The noise of Cody snoring might alert the Vietcong to the American presence. Bruno was so protective of Cody that he wouldn't let anybody near him during the nights. So out in the field Cody was always supposed to sleep with a rope tied around each leg: one rope attached at the other end to Bruno and one stretched out so that someone could pull it if the snoring grew too loud. That way, you could pull on Cody's leg and wake him without getting so close to him that Bruno would get protective.

Rick yawned. Because of the time change, it seemed like it had been daylight forever. There was some commotion at the window, but the guys in front of him had pressed so close, he couldn't see a thing. "Is that the Vietcong?" someone was saying.

The Vietcong were guerillas. Rick's father had explained all this to him, with the same kind of seriousness as when he'd first told Rick about girls and all that. He'd even drawn diagrams—both times! By definition, a guerilla was a kind of soldier, one who fought a stronger opponent—in this case the United States—by stealth and sabotage. The guerilla fighters hid in the jungles, blended in with the civilians, and even lived by the thousands underneath the ground in elaborate tunnels. Sarge was saying now, "You rarely see Charlie unless he's lying on his back dead. Sometimes you imagine you see him, though." Sarge turned suddenly and pointed to one of the big tires of the deuce-and-a-half. Rick turned quickly to where Sarge pointed. "Is Charlie behind that tire? Nah, that's just a shadow. Bam, bam, bam!" Sarge feigned getting shot. "No, that was Charlie after all."

In addition to fighting the Vietcong, the Americans were also fighting the NVA—North Vietnamese Army—but the NVA wore uniforms. The South Vietnamese Army was called the ARVN, for the Army of the Republic of Vietnam. Most of the enemy contact in Rick's area would be against the Vietcong, who used booby traps as one of their main weapons. The traps were psychological as well as physical weapons. Sarge said that if you let the traps get to you, then fear of stepping into one haunted every step you took. There could be booby traps everywhere. And that's what the dogs were for: to find the traps before any of the soldiers stepped in them.

Tan Son Nhut was both the American military air base and the civilian airport for Saigon. As the plane landed, Rick managed to get a glimpse of something on the tarmac. It looked like a red, white, and blue platform of some type. He wondered whether there was going to be some kind of welcoming ceremony. He couldn't wait to get Cracker out of the plane and into the fresh air. But when the doors opened, instead of fresh air, he felt a great wave of wet heat. All the guys leaned back at once, as if the heat had pushed them.

Still, Rick eagerly unloaded Cracker's crate and set it on the tarmac. He leaned his nose against the gate and felt his dog's wet nose push against his. "Cracker, good girl," he said. He heard laughing behind him and turned around. Some soldiers he didn't recognize were shaking their heads at Rick and his pals. "New guys!" one called out, laughing. "Give your doggie a kissie!"

Rick played it cool. Ignored 'em. That was a Scandinavian specialty. As he looked around, he saw what he'd thought was a welcoming stand: It was actually a pile of caskets lined up four high with flags draped over them. A couple of guys were already picking one up to take onto the plane that Rick had just gotten off of. U-Haul said, "Get ready to whip the world, soldier."

Rick didn't answer at first. But, hey, if he mouthed off, what were they going to do, send him to Vietnam? So he said to U-Haul, "Can't they wait until we're gone to do that stuff?" He deliberately left off the "Sergeant." He already felt a little less like a new guy, a little more like the rude guy his grandmother had seen.

U-Haul put his face in Rick's and said, "This. Is. A. War." Then he shouted to the men, "Empty that plane! Double-time!" They moved fast, climbing back on board to empty out the plane and make room for the caskets.

Twelve

So the 67th Infantry Platoon (Scout Dog) loaded up the trucks for the convoy to Bien Hoa. This was it. Rick and Cracker were about to become the best scout dog team in Vietnam.

Rick gawped as the convoy rode through Saigon. He'd never seen such chaos. Men dressed in what looked like black pajamas—exactly like the kind the enemy supposedly wore—rode bicycles so rickety, Rick would have thought they'd disintegrate under the weight of riders. The bicycles darted among the army trucks and the women balancing fruit—one basket hanging on each end of some kind of stick the women carried on their backs. Market owners and customers waved their arms and shouted; Rick assumed they were bartering. He could smell fish but couldn't see any. Kids ran barefoot alongside the truck screaming, "G.I. Joe!" He was surprised at how many Americans walked or rode through the streets. Rick and the rest of the squad sat in the back of a truck covered with their ponchos, their dogs huddled by their sides. The old-timers laughed and talked, but Rick just said over and over to himself, *I'm here.*

The air smelled different, like . . . like, well, he guessed the only thing in the world it smelled like was Saigon. He just hadn't expected it to smell so different in a different country. Sure, everyplace on the planet had trees, fruit, people, roads, and so on. He hadn't expected that a collection of trees, fruit, people, and roads could seem like a completely different planet.

The temperature was in the nineties that day, but because of the rain, Rick wasn't even sure whether he was sweating. He wiped water from his eyes and kept gawping.

As the convoy left Saigon, the guys quieted down. Rick peered at every shadow for Vietcong hiding along the road. Jungle loomed around them, palms and elephant grass and trees so thick, you couldn't see past the first layer. Mud splattered on their faces and filled every crevice in the road and every bomb crater in the fields. Rick's heart skipped a beat as a few old-timers suddenly pointed their rifles toward something, and then Rick saw a couple of young, crying kids run out of the jungle and away down the long, long road they'd just left behind.

The convoy rumbled through a village. Nobody spoke—it was as if they'd all realized at once that they were an open target. Anyone could be hiding any-where and fire on them. The civilian hootches were roofed with straw, and most were small—probably only one room. There was no concrete anywhere, just some tin and yellow thatch amid the green jungle that was everywhere. Cracker was pressed between Rick and Tristie.

"Feels like Disneyland, don't it?" a talkative black guy nicknamed "Uppy" finally said. He was an old-timer—just twenty-three years old but on his second tour of duty. His real name was Upton. He was one of the few old-timers who didn't make fun of the new guys. He was a shortish guy but looked like he could deadlift about five hundred pounds.

"Yeah," said Rick. "Except you don't get killed in Disneyland." Not that he'd ever been to Disneyland. Now he was a lot farther from home than California.

Rick didn't see any other trucks, but he did see

more men in those black pajamas riding bicycles. A couple of beautiful Vietnamese girls stood by watching Rick's truck work its way through the mud. Uppy leaned over and waved at the girls. "*Xin chào*, girls!" he called out.

Then one of girls looked straight at Rick and said, "I like! I like you! You number one!" He stared after her. Dang, she was choice!

Then he heard laughter from Uppy and a couple of the other seasoned soldiers who were hitching a ride in their truck. Uppy leaned out of the truck and shouted at the girl, "Hey, how about liking me?"

Cracker's head shot up. She smelled something— something important. *Chickens!* She saw chickens under a house and barked wildly, setting off a round of barking among all the dogs. The handlers pulled their leashes tight, and twenty-four voices called out at once: "No!"

Cracker gazed back longingly as the truck drove past. Those were perfectly good chickens. She looked at Rick and tried to explain: "Woof!"

Rick just shook his head. He waited for Sarge to yell at them to control their dogs, but for some reason, he didn't.

As they left the village area, nothing but jungle surrounded them again. Sarge's face took on falcon-like features as he peered into the jungle. "Any Vietcong around here?" Rick called out.

Sarge shook his head. "None reported. But that doesn't mean they're not there. We always say, 'They're everywhere and nowhere.'"

The convoy passed what looked like a destroyed village—a few half-standing huts in the rain—before turning down a winding road. After a few more hours of driving, Rick saw some sorry-looking buildings in the distance.

"That Bien Hoa?" he asked, disappointed.

Several times today Cracker had heard that word "Benwa."

"We've been temporarily reassigned" was all Sarge said. "This used to be a temporary FSB, but they're using it now for the 271st Airborne. We'll be supporting their ground infantry. There's been a lot of contact here lately."

Rick wasn't going to ask what the heck an "FSB" was. But he wished somebody else would. Finally, he whispered to Twenty-Twenty, "What's FSB?"

Twenty-Twenty whispered back, "Fire support base. Temporary camp they set up that sometimes becomes permanent."

When Rick's truck arrived at camp, he was even more disappointed. Even Cody seemed less than his usual jovial self. Camp was basically a flat, muddy plain with a bunch of ugly buildings and about ten thousand packed sandbags lying against them. Literally about ten thousand. Rick already knew exactly who was going to fill the sandbags around *their* hootch.

The trucks moved through the gates and stopped in front of a big, empty space. The dogs and handlers got off while Sarge talked to a major who'd approached the convoy. Rick liked watching the sarge kowtow to somebody else. Then Sarge walked over to where the men waited. He swept his hand toward the empty space. "Meet your new home, gentlemen!"

Rick and Twenty-Twenty glanced at each other. Finally, Cody asked, "Where are the barracks, Sergeant?"

The old-timers burst out laughing. "Man, oh, man," said one. "You gotta love new guys. Hey! Hey! If anyone is looking for the Holiday Inn, it's right over there." Then he and his buddies laughed again and walked off.

"We're going to build barracks," said Sarge. "That is, if we get the materials. In the meantime, we'll use the tents."

Rick asked, "Sarge, does that mean there are no dog kennels, either?"

"Ditto on the kennels, except for now we'll use the crates."

Rick watched Sarge look the platoon over. Naturally, Sarge's eyes stopped on him. "Lanski, you can start filling sandbags."

"Cody, you and Mason set up the tents."

Rick didn't listen to the rest. This was just great. His very first assignment in the Vietnam War was filling stinkin' sandbags. One of the old guys took pity on him and handed him a shovel so he wouldn't have to use his e-tool—the entrenching tool the men all carried. Rick stuck his shovel into the ground and lifted a load of dirt. All right, that wasn't so bad. The second one wasn't bad either. But by the time he'd finished just a few bags, his palms had already grown raw. He looked around the firebase at all the sandbags. On the upside, there were worse assignments—a couple of guys had been assigned to clean out the latrines.

Once in a while someone would walk by and he'd hear them say, "New guys." Blisters bubbled on his palms. Technically, these weren't sandbags, they were dirtbags, and right now the dirt was actually mud.

As Rick filled the bags, someone else piled them around their tents and the dog crates, but you could pile them only so high. A mortar attack from above could kill them. Someone had lined the crates up together, and Rick could see rain slanting into the crates. Rick wasn't supposed to, but he and some of the other guys also assigned to filling sandbags let their dogs off leash while they worked.

Rick spied an old-timer walking by and called out, "Say, man!"

The guy stopped. "Yeah?"

"Are there any extra tarps around? Our dogs are gonna get soaked while they're trying to sleep tonight." That is, if night ever came. The time change made Rick's head groggy. He squinted at the bright sky.

"Whatcha got to trade?"

"Aw, come on, we're all in the same army."

The guy shook his head and said what Rick knew he was going to say: "New guy."

Cody walked over. "I got a watch," he said.

Rick looked at Cody with surprise. That watch was his pride and joy.

The old-timer leaned over to study the watch. He tried to appear nonchalant, but Rick could see his eyes lighting up. Cody pulled it off his wrist. "It's solid gold," Cody told him. "My grandfather won it playing poker."

The old-timer said, "I seen better."

Rick knew a little about bargaining. Even with prices stuck to the items in the hardware store, sometimes people tried to negotiate. Now he looked nonchalant and said, "Forget it, we'll find someone else to trade with."

The old-timer scratched his cheek. "I'll tell you what. I'm gonna do you a favor 'cause you're new."

"We'll also want some steaks for dinner tonight," Rick said. "That watch is worth a lot of money."

"I'll talk to Mike," the old-timer said.

"Who's Mike?"

"You don't know Mike? Mike's the most important guy in camp. You gotta know Mike. He's just a spec four, but he's more important than a general as far as you're concerned. A general don't care if your dogs get wet, and a general ain't gonna get you no tarp *or* no steak. We call Mike our 'procurement specialist.'"

So later that day the dogs had their tarp stretched out on poles over their crates, Mike had the only thing of value Cody had ever owned, and the guys and their dogs ate steak for dinner. Cody was just about the most popular guy in Vietnam that night.

Rain poured for several days. After a while you accepted it, just like it was regular air. You walked through it like it was nothing. The dogs weren't as effective in rain because it washed away the smells, but Cody got called out on a mission anyway, to take a chopper to a drier area.

Rick spent most of the first four days filling sandbags, or mudbags. He gloved his hands to protect the blisters and attacked the mud and felt the opposite of the relaxation he felt in the shop at home, working with his dad's tools. He felt frustrated out here.

Since Cody had already gotten chosen to go out on a mission, it didn't seem fair that Rick was still filling these dang bags. What kind of high-tech helicopter war was this, anyway?

Then on the fifth day the skies cleared. During formation Sarge yelled out at him, "Hanski, you got a search and destroy."

"Tomorrow?"

"Now, mister."

The crazy thing was that even though Rick had been wanting his chance to whip the world, he now realized that it was a lot safer filling sandbags. Still, he couldn't wait to show off Cracker. As was customary with new handlers, one of the "short" handlers would accompany him. "Short" meant a soldier who had only a short time left in country, so they were called "short" or "short-timers." By tradition, short-timers worked mostly in the rear, which meant jobs as far from combat as possible. They'd also already turned in their dogs so that the dogs could learn to work and bond with new handlers. Some handlers thought giving up their dogs was one of the hardest parts of their jobs. Rick didn't like to think about it.

The mission was to make contact in an area where a reconnaissance team had said Charlie might be hiding. Rick heard that the team had reported some fresh bark scraped from a tree. Didn't sound like much of a lead to him, and probably didn't sound like much of a lead to anybody because the brass was sending out only a couple of small platoons.

Rick waited at the makeshift kennels while the short-timer sat with his former dog—a pure black German shepherd—talking to him. At one point the short-timer leaned his head into his dog's coat. Rick turned away; it seemed like a private moment. He patted Cracker's head. "We got a long way to go before I'm short."

Finally, the other handler left his dog, and they walked to the helicopter pad. They had just one cigarette between them, so they shared it.

"I guess you had a good dog?"

"He's the best dog in Vietnam. Name's Mack. He was one of the first dogs in country."

"Yeah, I noticed he's got white on his chin."

"Another handler is taking over, and then they'll probably retire Mack."

"You going to take him home eventually?"

"They won't let me."

"What happens when they retire a dog?"

The man looked into the distance and shook his head. "I dunno what's going to happen to him."

Then the pilots began arriving, and Rick, the short-timer, and Cracker hopped on a Huey. The short-timer sat with his legs hanging out the door-way—all the doors were taken off the choppers for faster loading and unloading. Rick had liked the chopper during training, but now in the back of his mind he couldn't shake the thought that this could be his last ride. There were five birds altogether, so this wasn't a big mission. He looked at Cracker, her face full of joy as the wind blew back her ears.

Cracker loved being on the helicopter. The wind pounding her face filled her with life. She was ready for anything.

The choppers landed ten minutes later, and the men leaped off. Rick counted about forty men. Everyone looked pretty relaxed. The commanding officer told Rick to head due east. Rick began walking point with Cracker and the other handler.

Cracker didn't like the other guy walking so close to them. A couple of times she growled at him, but then she felt the harness jerk and heard Rick snap, "No!" So she put up with the other man. She kept looking back at Rick to see if she was going to be let off leash, but Rick never gave any indication. The whole day they walked—and walked and walked and walked—through light brush. She didn't smell anything special, except the body odor of the guy walking next to Rick. Then she smelled gunpowder and pricked up her ears. The smell kind of twirled around in the air with the wind. She looked back at Rick, and he said, "Search." She walked more and then heard the whistle of the wind passing over string. She sat down.

"Whatcha got, girl? She's got something," said Rick. He didn't move forward—he'd learned his lesson well back in Georgia. He, the other handler, and Cracker fell back while one of the men checked out and then fired at the booby trap, setting it off. Cracker didn't even flinch at the explosion. Man, she was a great dog.

Rick found he loved walking point. This is what he'd been trained for. He thought again about saving that boy's life. He could save lives today, and he felt one hundred percent certain that Cracker wouldn't let him get killed. She found seven other booby traps that day. He'd heard the record was more than one hundred, but he didn't believe it. Rick thought it had been a pretty low-key day, but when they went back to the camp several guys from the mission nodded at him. Respect. It felt good. He snuck Cracker some extra food that night.

Cracker spent the night alone in her crate. She didn't understand why some nights she had to sleep by herself in the crate and some nights she slept outside with Rick. She liked to sleep with Rick, though she still vaguely remembered her bed with Willie. That bed was pretty comfortable. She did miss that a little. And the concrete they used to walk on was easier on the feet than these bumpy trails. On the other hand, she'd felt something out there in the bush today, something new that she hadn't felt even in that other place where they'd searched through the bushes. She felt like she was *herself*. That was strange, because "herself" really loved lying in a soft bed. But out there, searching for something she knew was important to Rick, and somehow also important to her, she was herself. She didn't feel ecstatic, like she did when Rick was petting and praising her, and she didn't feel excited, like when he was just about to feed her. She felt like she was herself and that she was a part of everything around her. It was something new. She liked it. And when she was finished for the day, she felt like she was Somebody Important. She knew Rick felt important too. They were important together.

When Rick returned, Twenty-Twenty and Cody were off on missions. He saw them less and less. They'd both pulled a couple of longer missions right away, and just as they got back, Rick pulled his second mission. It seemed that the handlers worked more independently than most guys. One of the short timers had said you usually didn't even know the men you were working with.

Rick's second mission was a night ambush near base. He went out with a platoon of twenty-four men. He and Cracker cleared the area first, meaning he walked through the area in an orderly fashion searching for booby traps or enemy mines. Cracker didn't alert a single time, and one of the guys grumbled that she "isn't finding anything." But Rick knew that she didn't alert because there was nothing to alert for. That night the platoon set up claymore mines around the perimeter of their nighttime defensive position. If any enemy soldiers approached in the night, they would be instantaneous BKs, if they were lucky. If they weren't lucky, they would be dead.

Ambushes were often set up in graveyards because they were above the water table. That way, you didn't have to lie in the wet all night as the water from nearby swamps or rice paddies rose with the tides. So there they were, sitting over bones, waiting for a fight. While it was still light, the men pretended to set up for the night. When darkness fell, they moved about one hundred yards away, to trick the V.C.

Rick was standing up when machine-gun fire broke the silence. He hit the dirt, then lifted his head and saw most of the guys laughing at him. A couple of other new guys had also hit the dirt. Then an old-timer told him, "That was an M-16." And as Rick replayed the sound in his head, he realized it *was* an M-16, meaning it was shot by a friendly. Charlie used AK-47s. The sergeant in basic training had shot one off for the guys, so Rick knew the difference. He felt like an idiot. Well, at least some of the other guys had done the same thing.

After they moved camp, Rick lay still in the darkness, listening for the other guys but not hearing them. These guys were pros.

Rick had done his work for the day and didn't have to take a watch. The world seemed peaceful, the breeze almost cool. This was war? He let himself drift off, Cracker pressed up against his legs. They weren't allowed to sleep on their ponchos that night because ponchos made a rustling noise and also reflected light. So he kept his poncho rolled up in his rucksack. Some guys didn't even bother to bring their ponchos. Cracker stood up and pulled lightly on her leash. Rick knew she wanted it off, but he felt too new to all this to take the chance.

Except for one almost-cool breeze Rick felt, the temperature didn't seem to drop at all during the night. But the clouds began to clear and the stars shone through. He slept well.

When morning came, the sky was completely clear for the first time since he got to Vietnam. Far in the distant plains Rick could see a huge, green cone with remnants of red cloud hovering at the tip. Above it the sky was blue. It was a lone mountain, rising above the plains and rice paddies. He'd heard of it: Nui Ba Den—Black Virgin Mountain—named for a woman whose fiancé had died.

Uppy took off his boots and peeled away long strips of skin off his feet.

"Aw, man, can't you do that in private?"

Uppy laughed. "Immersion foot. Wait'll you get it. It's from wearing damp boots all the time."

"I ain't getting no immersion foot," Rick said.

"How you gonna stop it?"

"Willpower," Rick said. Both men laughed. Rick could tell that Uppy was laughing *with* him. Uppy nodded toward a new guy who was taking out five pairs of neatly rolled socks, several pairs of boxers, and an extra shirt from his overloaded bag. The new guy picked out different clothes to put on, then stopped to swat wildly at some mosquitoes—Rick had already noticed that old-timers just waved them away or even ignored them. And he already knew that he'd rather stink and be filthy than carry extra clothes on his back. And then Rick *knew* he wasn't a new guy anymore.

Cracker stood up and shook herself off. She could hear the choppers in the distance. In a moment she saw everybody else getting up too.

Rick picked up his bag and waited. The ambush was a bust. No snipers, no V.C., no nothing. He'd heard that was usually the way it went. You set up an ambush or humped the bushes for hours, or even for days, and nothing happened. Then, every so often, you made contact. Some guys had been in country almost a year and had made contact only a handful of times. Other guys had had the bad luck to make contact a dozen times in three months. Rick wasn't sure now whether he wanted to make contact or not. So far Vietnam just seemed like some kind of bizarro alternate universe where the leaves were as big as a man and where you never saw the enemy.

He hopped on the Huey with Cracker and hung his legs out the door as they flew over the land. Cracker sat beside him, pressing against his arm.

Thirteen

ONE DAY CODY "REQUISITIONED" A POWER GENERATOR from a runway during a mission. The generator was just lying there unguarded, and Cody got a bunch of guys to help him carry it and throw it into a deuce-and-a-half. Nobody ever "stole" anything in Vietnam. Basically, if an item wasn't nailed down, it was fair game. So you could requisition said item, and instead of Sarge being mad at you, you would rise in his estimation. So the 67th IPSD had traded the generator for material for kennels and barracks, which the handlers spent the next week building and surrounding with sandbags.

Requisitioning was an important part of surviving in Vietnam. Mike was the base camp's procurement specialist, and the 67th IPSD had appointed

Twenty its personal procurement specialist—in country the guys often just shortened his name to "Twenty." Twenty took the generator to Mike and not only got the building material, but also snagged a case of Coke. He was a better bargainer than Cody—Cody would give away his grandmother for a tiny jar of foot fungus cream. Another good thing about Twenty-Twenty was that his uncle just happened to be a well-decorated lieutenant colonel who just happened to be stationed in Saigon, who just happened to have dined at the White House, and who just happened to think the world of Twenty. Twenty's uncle gave him a little extra bargaining power. Not a lot, because he couldn't go crying to his uncle about any little thing. But the guys knew that if it was really important, Uncle was always there. Rick took the case of Coke back to Mike. Mike was actually wearing a paper crown. The man was power crazy. But no question, he was the king of the base. "Mikey. How about some shingles for the doghouse roofs?"

Mike laughed. "Shingles? Just for a case of Coke? What do you think this is, Minnesota?"

"I'm from Wisconsin."

"Minnesota, Wisconsin, whatever—I ain't got shingles."

"Well, what else you got?" For crying out loud, why couldn't the guy just cooperate?

"Got some tin," Mike said.

"All right, just give me that. We'll make do."

Mike looked at him. "Dammit, I don't know why I feel sorry for you guys. The tin's on the house. Keep your Coke."

"Thanks!" Rick said. He paused, then added, "Nice crown."

The tools were hardly state of the art, but Rick was able to take charge. In fact, he preferred a regular saw to an electric one because he enjoyed working with his hands so much. He'd never been in charge of anything before, but all those tables he'd made really helped him build the kennels. They didn't have porches, but they did the job. It felt kind of good to be in charge after a lifetime of being simply a good worker. Anyway, now the dogs had nicer accommodations.

Cracker's kennel was next to Tristie's. She knew Rick had arranged that. She just knew, like she always knew when Rick, Cody, and Twenty-Twenty were coming before she saw them. She could smell them or hear them, or she would just know. Sometimes Bruno or Tristie knew first and would stand up and move to their gates. That was the sign for Cracker to move to her gate as well. So by the time the guys arrived, all three dogs would be sitting at the front of their kennels, waiting. Their guys always showed up first, and then Cracker, Bruno, and Tristie liked to jump around their kennels in celebration. They had the best guys.

The next assignment Rick pulled freaked him out: He'd be walking point in front of an entire company of 150 men. One hundred fifty! He remembered that night at the dinner table when he'd told his family he wanted to whip the world. Pretty easy to say in a frame house in a town in Wisconsin. Now he figured that, just in case, he should drop his parents a line. He wrote only that he was going out on his first big mission and that he'd write more later. Then he figured it was better not to worry them and tore up the letter.

That evening Rick brushed Cracker twice, murmuring her favorite words—"good girl"—the whole time. Then he told her, "We're going to have a whole company following us. This is big stuff." Over and over he said, "It's big stuff, girl, big stuff." But he didn't know whether that was true. It could be another dud.

In the late afternoon Cody and Twenty both got back from the field looking like, well, like they just got back from a war. They didn't say a word through dinner and left the mess hall immediately. Nobody spoke as they walked to the kennels.

Instead of sitting among the trees like they usually did, they all sat behind a warehouse. Cracker galloped to where Bruno and Tristie were chasing rats in a rice paddy. In the distance Rick watched some locals going through the base garbage dump. Cody stuck a piece of gum in his mouth. Twenty-Twenty lit a cigarette. Both seemed deep in thought.

"So what's up, man?" Rick finally asked.

Twenty took a breath and nodded for a few seconds, as if thinking. "It was confusing out there," he said at last. "You can't tell which of the indigenous personnel are friendlies and which aren't." He lowered his voice as some Vietnamese the army had hired to do laundry walked past. "You don't know who to trust. The villagers look just like Charlie." One original aim of the United States had been to "win the hearts and minds" of the villagers. But that all seemed to be in the past now. "I shot a Vietcong girl. I mean, she was armed—she aimed a rifle at me—but, you know, I didn't really expect to be fighting girls."

"You shot a *girl?*" said Rick. He'd heard that a lot of girls fought for the Vietcong, but to shoot one. . . .

Twenty-Twenty turned angrily to Rick. "You weren't there, you know?"

"Easy, man, I didn't mean anything."

Cody, frowning, said, "If she was gonna kill you, you gotta protect yourself."

"Yeah, I know." Twenty-Twenty leaned his head back against the wall. The dogs were freaking out over a rat. Twenty smiled at Tristie barking and hopping around. "She's the only worthwhile thing in this war."

Bruno ran over just to say hi to Cody. Even he looked different. He'd always been the oldest dog in the squad, but now Rick noticed white hairs on his nose that he'd never noticed before.

Rick spied some more rats sticking their heads up in the field. "Hey, let's pop some rats." He'd seen some old-timers do it when they needed a little tension release.

Cody and Twenty seemed unsure, but then Cody smiled and said, "Yeah! Those damn rats are driving me nuts. I saw one in the mess hall the other day!" Then it was like old times again.

Rick got blasting caps and cheese, and he, Twenty-Twenty, and Cody walked into the field laughing. The dogs went crazy—Cracker even managed to grab a big rat in her mouth and shake it dead. "Good girl!"

Rick called out. He had a wiener in his pocket that he had been planning to give her later. His mother had been sending him five dollars now and then, and he'd been using the money to buy hot dogs for Cracker from Mike. He gave her a piece of one now. Then he placed cheese on a couple of blasting caps and jogged off to watch with Twenty and Cody.

They called their dogs to them. The dogs obeyed, Cracker the most reluctantly. She kept looking back over her shoulder at the paddy. A moment later a huge rat jumped on a blasting cap. *Boom!* Cracker and Tristie danced the happy dance.

"Soldiers!"

The guys jumped up. Jeez! It was the captain! Rick had never even talked to the captain. He and his friends stood stiff, dogs at their sides.

"May I ask what you're doing?" the captain asked, in a voice that implied he knew perfectly well what they were doing. Fortunately, he was standing in front of Twenty-Twenty.

Twenty-Twenty said, "Sir! We noticed that the rodent population was becoming problematic, sir! The rodent population has gotten so brazen that they sometimes walk right into the mess hall while we're eating, sir! And we decided to resolve the problem! Sir! And—"

"That's enough, Private. I want all your names."

Twenty-Twenty said, "My name is Brian Butler, sir. You may know my uncle, Lieutenant Colonel Brian Butler, after whom I was named and who, uh, whom, by the way, was awarded two Silver Stars, the Distinguished Flying Cross, eleven Air Medals, and the Legion of Merit."

The captain paused. "Brian Butler?" He paused again. "All right, just pick up any unexploded caps in the field, and—and I don't want to see you wasting good ammunition on any more rats."

Later that night the handlers' barrack was nearly empty, with most of the guys out on missions. Rick thought about how different Cody and Twenty-Twenty were than they had been a week ago. They seemed older. The clearest way he could tell they were different was because he knew he hadn't changed, but he could tell he didn't quite fit in with them anymore. And Cody didn't seem as upbeat as he used to. Rick wondered if he himself would be different a week or two from now.

Monsoon season was in full force, and the winds howled and rain poured. Rick listened to it pound on the roof that night. Even in the darkness, he could feel that Twenty-Twenty was awake. "Twenty-Twenty!" he said.

"Yeah."

"You saved our butts. But I thought you were named Orrin after your grandfather."

"Yeah, I was."

Rick closed his eyes. He hoped Cracker was getting a good rest.

Actually, Cracker was still awake, thinking of Rick. A trickle of rainwater ran through her kennel. She moved to avoid it. She heard rat-a-tat noises in the distance. They were different from the noises Rick's gun made. Inside the kennel, the trickle seemed to be following her. She moved again and sighed as she laid down her head.

The next morning Rick showed up again. She stood very still. She could feel how nervous he was, like his blood was tingling, and that made her nervous. She wondered what it was that was making their blood tingle together.

"This is it, Cracker."

Cracker stared straight at him. She knew exactly what he was saying—namely, that something important was happening and that it was happening to them both together. She felt so eager to please him that when he opened up the gate, she spun around several times chasing her tail before she could bring herself to sit in front of him.

Another soldier came by and stood next to them. "This the dog?" he said.

"Cracker," Rick said, and Cracker wagged her tail. "Cracker's the best dog in Vietnam."

The other soldier narrowed his eyes as Cracker hopped around chasing herself. "She better be, because we're going to a hot zone."

"Hot zone." Cracker had heard that while they were running around before the long trip over here. Whenever there was gunfire in the air or men hidden in bushes, Rick would lean in and say, "Hot zone." She listened now but didn't hear any gunfire. She looked up at Rick to ask him about the hot zone. He didn't say anything, just slung his sack on his back and walked with the other soldier to where a chopper was already waiting, its blades whirring. At the chopper he knelt next to her and leaned toward one of her ears. "You–are–the–best–dog–in–Vietnam!" Rick shouted. "Do you understand?"

Dog! She wagged her tail.

"We're heading south, toward Bien Hoa. But not quite that far."

Benwa!

Rick saw that a couple dozen choppers had already taken off and more were landing to pick up soldiers. Man, he'd never seen so many choppers in the air at once. They were gonna kick some butt! He also saw some Cobra gunships—nicknamed "Sharks" or "Redbirds"—circling in the distance, their front ends painted with red and white shark's teeth.

After half a dozen other men had boarded the chopper, he and Cracker climbed on. Rick hunched over and avoided the back, even though the top blades whirled at least a foot above his head and the rear blades churned several feet away. As he climbed aboard, he suddenly had a funny feeling: He didn't feel like *him*. That is, he knew he was him, and he knew it was him climbing onto the chopper, but he didn't quite feel as if he were there. Yet he didn't feel as if he were anywhere else, either. It was just that he had expected this moment to feel intense, and instead, it felt far away.

Rick took a place in the center and sat with Cracker. The other men looked curiously at her. A couple of them smiled and petted her. Cracker leaned her nose out the open door, but Rick pulled her back hard. "No!" He knew the centrifugal force would keep her in, but he wanted to be extra safe today. She lay next to him as the bird lifted off. The whole sky was roaring.

Someone said, "Hey, dog man. I hope you're smiling when this is over!" Rick realized he'd been half grinning, and he probably looked stupid. He was grinning more from nervousness than anything else. His first hot zone!

As they rose, nobody spoke. Rick didn't know any of the guys on board, but they looked like they'd been here awhile. There was something different in their eyes. Down below in the fields Rick saw the bomb craters, some of them filled with dirty water. From a heavy forest beyond a rice paddy, smoke exploded upward. Rick took a big breath and said into Cracker's ear, "I hope that's not where we're going."

But they went on, the thunder in Rick's ears starting to seem normal. Every so often he'd see a fist of smoke shoot upward from the ground. Suddenly, the chopper started to descend, hovering above a rice paddy. The men began to jump out. Then Rick had the feeling he'd been expecting, like he was here. *Really* here. Like this was it. His heart pounded hard, and his whole body felt as if it were quivering. He started to hop out, and Cracker launched off at the same time, flying past him.

"No!" he shouted, too late. Cracker was already hurtling forward, sailing to the end of her leash. The leash snapped taut, and Rick slammed facedown in the stagnant water. By the time he righted himself, the helicopter had lifted away, and everybody was laughing at him.

"Claimed he had the best dog in Vietnam," he heard someone say.

Rick wiped the water from his face, furious. Bad, bad first impression. Very bad. Another chopper hovered, and more men jumped off.

"Dog Handler!" the lieutenant called out.

"Yes, sir!" Rick shouted, his voice sounding louder than he had meant it to.

"Southeast, Dog Handler!"

"Yes, sir!" He thought about adding, *My name is Hanski, sir,* but decided not to. "Cracker, search!"

They were on what was officially called a "search-and-destroy mission." Unofficially, "find 'em and fix 'em." A reconnaissance patrol believed there might be enemy in this area. The mission now was to find Charlie or anything that might help him and destroy it. It also meant that if they made contact, they were to kill the enemy—"fix 'em."

Cracker sniffed the air. She leaned her head left, then right, as smells drifted through her nostrils. Her ears flickered once, but just at the newness of the situation.

Rick wondered whether that flicker was enough for him to stop the 150 guys behind him. He decided not, and they trudged on for a few more minutes.

Cracker raised her head and turned it more south than east. Her ears stood up straight. That was a definite alert. Rick turned to Rafael, the guy walking behind him. He moved his fingers in a kind of short wave. Rafael was Rick's slack man, but this was the first time they'd worked together. Funny to think that two guys who hadn't known each other the day before now depended on each other for their lives. Rafael hurried up beside Rick. "What's she got?" Rafael asked in a low voice.

"I dunno. She's alerting south. It's definite, but not immediate. I mean, it's not like the enemy is two feet away. But it's definitely people, not mechanical. She sits for booby traps."

Rafael had just left to report to the company leader when a gunshot fired. Rick knew immediately that it was an AK-47—he didn't make the same mistake twice. Everybody's legs dropped out from under them, water from the rice paddy splashing upward. Rick and Cracker lay flat behind a low dike, men close on either side of them. The adrenaline made Rick's skin buzz. His mind felt clearer than it had felt, maybe ever. He figured the shot had come from the south, and when he looked down the row, he saw other men aiming their guns in that direction. "Down, Cracker," he said, though she was already down.

The man to the left of him asked in a low voice, "How many are there?" He eyed Cracker.

Rick had noticed that some of the guys who weren't familiar with scout dog teams seemed to think that the handlers could read the dogs' minds.

"Uh, I don't know."

Another gunshot sounded, followed closely by yet another. The shots seemed to come from two different directions.

"At least two," the man on the right said.

Rick heard the radioman behind him.

"Alpha, Alpha, this is Ranger. We got two bad guys firing small arms." He gave their coordinates and asked for support. "Do you copy?"

Rick could hardly hear the reply. It sounded like mostly static over the radio, but then he heard their radioman say, "That's a 10-4."

They didn't move. Nobody moved, but like all the guys, Rick held his M-16 low and ready. Rick was proud of how well behaved Cracker was. Her leash lay under the water somewhere. Cracker lay still but alert. Rick's foot went to sleep. Then a hand went to sleep. Sometimes the fire seemed to be coming from different directions, but never from more than two at once. Rick lay with the left side of his face immersed in water. Cracker tried to lap at the water, and Rick hissed, "No." If she drank this stagnant water, she might get sick. But he couldn't get to a canteen right now.

At one point Cracker moved her nose forward and pushed at his face under the water. He reached under the water and felt something slimy attached to his cheek. He couldn't stop himself from trying to see what was there. He slowly turned his head until he could see something black bulging from it. A leech.

For some insane reason, the leech made him almost laugh out loud. It made him think of how crazy it would be to die out here, with a leech attached to his cheek.

Cracker suddenly leapt straight up in the air, almost as if somebody had picked her up and thrown her. She splashed down in the water. He frowned at her as she leapt up again. A shot whizzed by. She splashed down.

"Down," Rick whispered urgently. A shot hit the dike right on the other side of where they lay. Rick felt something bite at him and nearly jumped himself.

The soldiers on either side of them started inching away as another shot whizzed over Rick's head. The soldiers kept inching away until only he and Cracker remained. Cracker looked at Rick desperately as she jumped into the air again. Rick tried to hold his gun with one hand and grab her paws with the other. "Down. Stay. Stay down."

He heard a staticky voice over the radio, then the reply from his radioman: "That's a 10-4. Fire when ready."

Someone called out, "Take cover! Incoming!"

Rick saw the smoke from the mortar fire—it looked about twenty meters away. He heard the radio guy again: "Alpha, Alpha, this is Ranger! Move one half klick to the south! Do you copy?"

The fire ceased immediately, then resumed farther to the south. A "klick" was a kilometer.

Someone hissed from Rick's right. The lieutenant was signaling him to move. Rick gave Cracker the crawl gesture, and they slithered through the water. The other soldiers were also slithering along. Every so often one of them must have inadvertently raised his body too high, for a shot would explode into the air ahead of or behind Rick. So the snipers no doubt knew the company was on the move. But after more mortar fire, the snipers fell silent.

One by one the men crawled through the nipa

palms circling the paddy. They kept crawling until they reached the cover of the jungle. It was only there that Rick allowed Cracker to stand up. Rick reached to pull the leech off his cheek. "Don't touch it!" Rafael said. "They leave their jaws embedded in your flesh if you try to pull them off. You gotta make them let go with a cigarette or bug juice."

The men were all drenched. Rick knelt to check Cracker. A leech dangled from her belly. Maybe that's what had caused her to jump up, although he'd heard leeches released anesthetic so you didn't feel it when they bit you, or even when they hung on for hours.

Someone tapped his shoulder and nodded toward where the lieutenant, water dripping from his face, was signaling Rick to come forward. Rick and Cracker hurried over. "Take the point, Dog Handler. If those snipers are still alive, let's fix 'em."

The adrenaline had drained from Rick. He was exhausted. He didn't even care about the leech on his cheek anymore. He still felt bad for Cracker, but he knew he couldn't take the time to pull off her leeches or his own. "Yes, sir," he said. He put on Cracker's harness and tried to sound calm yet urgent. "Search, Cracker. Search."

Fourteen

CRACKER WAS THIRSTY. SHE LOOKED AT RICK AND sent him the thought, but he just repeated, "Search!" Some of the leaves in the jungle were bigger than her. She stopped a moment to sniff a leaf, just because it was strange and big. It was as if she'd shrunk. She had a vague notion that Rick wouldn't understand why she was sniffing at it, but she had to know: What kind of thing was this huge leaf?

Rick caught up with her and squatted beside her. "Got something? Whatcha got?"

Nothing, actually. She lifted her nose to the air and breathed deeply, the way she did when she wanted to know what was going on. This was different from the way she took in air when she was just breathing. All she knew was that the air went someplace different when she was just breathing versus when she was trying to figure out a scent. A huge variety of new smells traveled back through her nose and filled her head. Her head was so filled with these smells that she kind of *became* them for a moment, just like she sometimes kind of became Rick. She realized he was still waiting for her. She wagged her tail at him, then walked away. He fell back; she knew where he was without even looking at him.

All of a sudden Cracker heard a noise that sounded like a really loud squirrel. She pulled toward the noise while Rick called, "Stay! Stay!" It was too late—Rafael was running forward, and all the men were holding their guns and aiming toward where Cracker was pointing. Rick spotted a monkey swinging away in the distance.

Rafael hissed, "What is it?"

"Monkey. It's nothing."

"You just about gave the whole company a heart attack." Rick could hear Rafael swearing to himself as he fell back.

Rick wanted to jerk on Cracker's harness, but dogs didn't understand a correction unless it came directly after an infraction. Instead, he knelt in front of her and met her eyes. "This is serious. Okay?"

Jungle foliage kept pricking at Rick, but he rolled

up his sleeves anyway. Some of the guys had taken off their shirts. Scratches already covered their bodies, but it was better than passing out from the heat.

A trail had already been worn through the forest. Cracker smelled other people on the trail, but not like the people Rick knew. A couple of times one of those black sticky things dropped onto her from the leaves above, and she quickly shook it off.

Rick didn't take his eyes off her. He'd heard that leeches sensed soldiers' heat and movement and would let go of the leaves when you walked through a forest. Every now and then several at once rained down in Rick's path. He could hear them dropping behind him, too.

He stopped just once to glance back. He wasn't supposed to take his eyes off Cracker, but for a minute there, the men moved so quietly that he doubted anybody was following him. It was spooky as hell that 150 guys could move so silently. That meant the enemy could do the same. Rafael trailed him by about seven yards, and behind that the men walked single file down the trail. They never bunched up. When Rick turned back around, Cracker's ears were flickering.

Intensity and focus washed through Rick. He felt about a thousand times more focused than he could ever remember feeling during training. Cracker didn't stop walking after her ears flickered, and Rick decided her alert hadn't been strong enough to stop the whole company.

Her ears flickered again, and again Rick debated halting everybody. But Cracker kept walking, so he kept walking. This was so different from training. Now he had to interpret Cracker even more exactly, had to understand precisely what each flick of her ears meant. Otherwise, if he stopped the company too often, they might think he was crying wolf and not take Cracker seriously. And if he didn't stop the company when there was real danger, men might die. He felt sick to his stomach. When he'd saved that kid's life a long time ago, he'd had no time to think. Now time seemed endless. The lives of all these men, of himself, and of Cracker depended on how well he understood the meaning of Cracker's every movement. He knew that if he failed, he would be tormented by guilt for the rest of his life. But the moment passed, and he was concentrating on Cracker again. Every so often one of her ears flicked, but that was probably because of a mosquito or small bug that he couldn't see.

They covered only about one hundred yards in twenty minutes, which Rick had heard was pretty standard for a hot area in heavy jungle. Boy, he never would have guessed it would be such hard work just studying his dog. Once in a while she would stop to meet eyes with him. He knew that the entire company was staring at them. Then, after one such meeting of eyes, she abruptly sat, almost as if Rick had commanded her to do so. Rick felt so shocked, he retched. He hurried to her but made sure not to pass her. He knelt down. "Whatcha got, Cracker? Whatcha got?"

Cracker knew exactly what "wachagah" meant. She turned to look at the ground in front of them, then turned back patiently to Rick.

Rick stared at the ground. He didn't see anything but a bunch of dead leaves. Slowly, half an inch at a time, he raised his eyes, searching out a trip wire. He did that twice but didn't see a wire. He didn't know what to do. He didn't see anything out of the ordinary. He even tried sniffing the air, as if that might help. He wondered whether he should turn and signal Rafael to come forward. He knew everybody was watching him and Cracker, waiting for a signal from him.

What should he do? *All right. All right.* This time he started out about ten feet in the air, then slowly moved his eyes down searching for the trip wire.

He still didn't see anything. He looked at Cracker. She met his eyes, then turned her nose toward the ground and sniffed lightly without moving her body.

He stared at the ground. Then he saw it. One leaf—really only one—didn't quite match the surrounding leaves. He looked around and spotted a bush deeper in the jungle. The leaves of that bush matched the one on the ground. It could mean nothing. It could mean only that a leaf from deeper in the jungle had fallen off and, over time, had migrated to right here. Cracker turned to the ground again and sniffed over it, then turned to him. Rick gestured Rafael forward.

Rafael walked quickly to them, but Rick kept him from moving past Cracker. Rafael said, "I don't see anything. What does she got?"

"I'm not sure. Look at that leaf. It looks out of place."

Rafael looked dubious, so Rick said, "She smells something too."

Rafael moved back to tell the lieutenant about it.

Rick petted Cracker and whispered, "Hope you got something, girl, or we're about to be embarrassed."

In a moment a soldier whose name Rick didn't even know knelt on the ground beside him. "I don't see anything," the soldier snapped.

151

Rick snapped back, "People see what they want. Dogs see what they see." That was a line Rick heard Cody use sometimes. Humans saw in wholes, not in pieces. They saw a total picture, colored by what they believed. Dogs used their senses to "see" all the details, uncolored by expectations and beliefs.

"Fall back, Dog Handler," the soldier commanded.

Rick and Cracker walked back and turned to watch as the soldier studied the leaves. In a moment the soldier gingerly cleared away a couple of leaves, then more and more. Rick saw that the leaves were covering a hole in the ground. The soldier hurried back to confer with the lieutenant, who sent word to Rick that it was a punji pit. Rick asked for permission to look at it.

He and Cracker stepped forward and stared into the pit. It was a tiny thing, about a foot deep and two feet square. Sharpened bamboo sticks stuck up from the ground and angled upward from the sides. He'd heard that sometimes guys jumped out of helicopters and landed right in one of these pits. The points of the sticks were brown, probably covered with human feces so that they would not only stab you, but infect you as well.

Cracker glanced into the pit. It looked like one of the pits she'd seen back in . . . wherever they'd been before—"Forbenning." She shook herself, and she could sense something hanging on her belly. And something was stuck in one of her paws. She couldn't feel it exactly, she just knew something was there. And she was still thirsty. And her stomach felt uneasy. She glanced at Rick. The glance made her forget the thing hanging from her belly, and even her thirst. He was staring right at her. "Good girl," he said. She pushed her nose under his hand for some petting. He petted her but not enough, so she pushed her nose under his hand again.

Rick removed Cracker's leeches while someone destroyed the pit. He used his bug juice rather than a cigarette so that if Cracker moved, she wouldn't get burned. He fingered bug juice on the black creature on her paw, and it fell right off. Same with the one on her belly and a third he found inside her thigh. He wanted to blast the leeches with his rifle. Instead, he touched the juice to the leech on his cheek, and it, too, fell to the ground, fat with his blood. He watched his blood trickle out of the leech. Then he felt all up and down Cracker to see if there were any more.

Rick knew Cracker had just earned some respect points. He could see it in the way everybody was looking at him and his dog. He knelt beside her and said softly, "Good girl, *good girl.*" After Rick gave Cracker some water, he turned to her and said, "Search, Cracker. Search!"

Cracker turned to the trail and lifted her snout, pulling scents to the back of her nose. She tilted her snout a bit more to catch a particular scent. She pricked her ears slightly. There was the slight suggestion of something, but she couldn't quite capture it. She waved her nose left and right, trying to find a place where the scent was stronger. But she couldn't quite get it.

She took a few steps forward. The scent got stronger, and it seemed to be associated with a sound. She rotated her ears toward the noise. It sounded like—no, it was gone.

She glanced at Rick and kept walking. She didn't know how much time passed. She just knew there were many smells, and some of them were very strong, but the one she was focused on wasn't very strong. The wind gusted, and she stopped. There it was, and now it was strong. She raised the hair on the back of her neck.

A little more sunshine than before had managed to reach through the canopy. Rick liked that: less creepy. Still, his heart beat hard when he saw the hair on Cracker's neck rise. But he didn't feel sick this time, just extra alert. Cracker pointed her nose at some thick bushes about thirty yards away.

Rick turned to Rafael and nodded three times. They'd decided that would be the signal when Cracker gave a strong human alert. The slack man sent word down the line. Rick saw soldier after soldier whisper to each other, until word reached the lieutenant. Then soldier after soldier sent word back up. Rafael signaled Rick to fall back.

Rick wanted to be the one who would get to take a prisoner, if there was one, but he knew that wasn't his job. Then as he watched the soldiers creep toward the bush, he felt a brief worry that maybe somebody innocent was hiding behind the bush.

Cracker followed Rick back as several other soldiers moved forward. She felt pretty excited. She knew there was somebody behind those bushes. It was exactly like so often before, when she and Rick had been in that other place. She recoiled slightly at something in the air. It was familiar from the other place, but she forgot the word Rick had called it. Her eyes stung a bit. Rick knelt next to her and murmured, "Tear gas."

Then it seemed the whole world was shooting and shouting. *Bam! Bam! Bam, bam, bam!* "Get him!" "Did you get him?" "Got him!" "Watch out!"

Rick hit the dirt, holding Cracker down. Then, sudden silence, broken when someone from in front shouted, "Medic!"

Someone else cried out, "Call for the dust-off!" A "dust-off" was a helicopter to take out the wounded. That meant at least one of their guys had gotten hit.

As the medic rushed forward, Rick overheard someone saying a sniper had been killed. A couple of soldiers had been wounded, one of them badly. In a minute, men rushed by carrying that soldier, blood already seeping through a bandage on his face. Rick didn't know his name. It was better that way. Another soldier had gotten hit in the arm. He walked by, his arm in a sling. He nodded at Rick and winked at Cracker as he moved past.

Their mission had been to find 'em and fix 'em, but they'd caught a sniper instead. Still, that was a big success. It was getting late. The lieutenant decided to head back, but he let the men take time to remove their leeches. Rick was surprised to see the men pull down their fatigues. *Aw, man.* Leeches stuck to guys all over the place. Rick pulled down his pants and saw a big, fat leech right between his legs. *AW, MAN!* He had to decide: Did he want to apply bug juice or a cigarette to the leech between his legs? He chose bug juice and watched the leech fall to the ground. Cracker growled at it.

Whenever the other guys happened to make eye contact with Rick, they nodded. Yessir, Rick and Cracker had racked up a lot of respect points today. He didn't expect any more remarks about being a new guy.

He saw Rafael take off his boots. One of Rafael's socks was bright red with blood. A leech must have gotten down his boot, then been squished. Rick had heard that it happened all the time. Those leeches could get anywhere. Insidious little freaks. The medic stopped by with a cigarette hanging from his mouth. He took out another cigarette, lit it, and handed it to Rick.

"Thanks, Doc," said Rick.

Doc nodded, then petted Cracker.

Cracker felt the man massage her head. "Good girl," he said. That felt nice—but not nearly as nice as when Rick did it.

Fifteen

CRACKER RAN AS FAST AS SHE COULD. HER MUSCLES had gotten stronger every day, and she loved to feel their power as she pushed off the ground to gallop. If she got caught, there would be a lot of trouble. So despite a nearly overwhelming desire, she didn't stop to eat the steak she had clenched in her jaws, just ran as fast as she could. Tristie raced by her side, and a few other dogs ran behind them. The calls of the men grew farther and farther away. She spotted a row of tall cans in front of her. Smelled like gas cans. Right before she reached the cans, she pushed up on her back legs as hard as she could and felt herself soar into the air. But she never forgot to keep her mouth clamped. She knew she would make it; she cleared the cans by such a small amount that her back paws brushed them as she landed. She stopped for one second and swallowed the steak.

By the time the other dogs reached her, the steak was gone. She could hear yelling in the background. The noisy man yelled loudest of all. She hung her head low as the noisy man and all the other men ran around the cans. They smelled of sweat. Rick marched up to her. She hung her head even lower and whined. She lifted her eyes lovingly and pawed at Rick. Before Rick could say a word, the noisy man spoke up. "That was *your* dinner, mister. I've told you guys to keep those dogs on a leash."

In the short time Cracker had been here, she'd noticed a change in the way Rick treated the noisy man. Rick was a lot more casual with him. Now he said, "Uh-huh, Sergeant," all the while glaring at Cracker.

Twenty had managed to procure some steak by trading a pile of choice magazines he'd obtained from somewhere. Who knew where he got the stuff he traded? That was one of his specialties. Twenty had specialties, focuses. No generalist there.

The men pulled the dogs by their collars into the kennels. Rick pushed Cracker in and said, "Bad girl! I'll see you tomorrow. No supper." He walked off. Cracker looked around. Every dog was staring at her.

She regurgitated the steak and sniffed at it. *Mmmm.* Smelled good. Very good. Then she swallowed it again and lay in the place where the setting sun slanted over the gated side of her kennel. She watched Rick's back retreat into the distance. She liked steak. *Very, very good.* She closed her eyes and let the sun warm her face. Every day was pretty good. Sometimes Rick took her out to work. The days were mostly dry. The temperatures were pleasant in the mornings and evenings, but when she worked in the afternoons, she got hot. Whenever she tried to drink from anyplace except Rick's steel pot or her bowl, he got mad at her. Right now she lapped up water from her bowl before lying in the sun again to fall asleep.

The next morning Rick showed up as usual with her breakfast. He fed her sullenly and left. She whimpered, and he turned around. She gave him a love look. "It's not funny," he said. "The whole unit got steak for dinner last night, and I got C rats."

C rats, mmmm. Good. Rick looked at her sternly, but she just wagged her tail. Then he cracked a smile and said, "Okay, let's go."

They spent the day with some other guys and dogs, jumping over the walls and through tunnels at the obstacle course the men had erected for the dogs to do what Cracker thought of as playacting. It was fun but not as intense as when they went out to work for real. The guys laughed more, and Cracker couldn't feel much tension, except maybe a certain competitiveness among Rick and his friends. She tried to do everything he said really well. Still, she knew these days were just pretend. Once, she raced ahead of Rick without any command from him and did the whole obstacle course. Then she ran up to him and sat. She waited for his reaction and got what she wanted. A smile. A "good girl."

Cracker loved playing. And every time she worked for real, more and more guys petted her and gave her food. Sometimes she could tell this annoyed Rick. He would say, "I'm her handler," which Cracker took to mean that he felt jealous, so then she would sit next to him or lick his hand to let him know she understood. But she still liked the treats.

During the evenings Rick would brush her and tell her she was the best dog in Nam. She would hear the exact same words coming from the mouths of Cody and Twenty as they brushed their dogs. She didn't know what the words meant, but she took them to mean "good dog."

Sometimes, even on the slow days, something would happen that would remind Rick that men were dying out there. Like once, he saw some guys gathered around a radioman. Rick heard shouting and screaming. The shouting, he realized, had come over the radio and from a different unit. He heard a man scream in pain. He looked around him. Here in his little section of the war everything was peaceful. But he was hearing someone over the radio, screaming, maybe dying. He listened soberly to the sounds of battle. He heard the screaming die out, and he wondered whether that meant the soldier was better . . . or worse.

Over the next few weeks Rick pulled some routine missions, or maybe Cracker was such a good dog that she made everything go smoothly. They cleared a couple of villages—where Cracker found some ammo and V.C. food caches—and they set up a few ambushes during which the most exciting thing that happened was that Rick got so many mosquito bites, it looked like he had a rash on his arms. Clearing villages was pretty routine. You just emptied the village of humans and animals and took your dog through looking for weapons or food caches. The first time was hard because Cracker got real interested in the chickens and other animals that the villagers kept, and Rick couldn't keep her focused. She didn't seem to understand that she wasn't supposed to chase small animals. Rick remembered how much she'd drooled when she'd seen the chicken at Fort Benning. Still, he felt he'd been able to control her pretty well here in country. Some of the dogs were even worse.

Every time they'd cleared a village here in Vietnam, she'd managed to find a few tunnels, but none of them seemed like V.C. tunnels. They were just the same old tunnels all the villagers dug to hide out in whenever the need arose. Nearly all the homes had double walls or secret tunnels. There were American soldiers called "tunnel rats" who specialized in exploring the more elaborate tunnels, when they could find them. Charlie had dug an elaborate system of tunnels throughout some areas of Vietnam. Nobody was sure exactly how elaborate the tunnels were, but it was rumored that thousands of people, even kids, lived underground. They slept, cooked dinner, went to school, planned attacks, all in the tunnels. Some of them didn't see daylight for months at a time, and some came out only at night to stage ambushes, or even to work the rice paddies. All this was utterly amazing to Rick. One guy in his neighborhood back home had built a bomb shelter in his backyard and had actually tried it out for a week. Rick's grandmother had said the guy was nutty as popcorn. Rick smiled as he remembered thinking that "nutty as popcorn" made no sense at all. Kind of like Twenty's "for all intensive purposes." The memory made him ache for home. Even for working in the hardware store.

It was hard for Rick to imagine living in a bomb shelter for a week, let alone a tunnel for several months. He couldn't imagine Cracker doing it either. Would probably drive her insane.

One day when things were especially quiet, one of the cooks declared that he could heat up an entire mess hall's worth of food in five minutes. "Watch this," said the cook. "I'm gonna revolutionize this army." Rick and Cody hung around for the show.

The cook took a thirty-two-gallon galvanized trash can and set it on three big food cans. He filled the big trash can with hot water and placed a stick of C-4 explosive under the can and lit it. It burned with a very hot and intense orange flame.

Cody, ever the optimist, said, "Hey, this might really work."

As the water boiled, the can started to shake violently. "It's gonna blow!" shouted Rick. He and the other guys took off and hit the dirt about twenty yards away, turning to watch the shaking can fall off its perch. The whole thing exploded, sending the can, food, and water in all directions. A captain appeared about thirty seconds later to chew out the cook. Every fly from Three Corps already seemed to be invading the area. The captain glared at all the men, who were now at attention. "None of you will be eating lunch today unless you care to partake in that food with the flies." Rick wanted to protest—when something like that was going on, of course you were going to watch. But he wasn't about to argue with a captain.

Even Cracker heard the explosion from her kennel. She could tell it was nearby, and she felt a surge of worry about Rick. She didn't see him again until that evening, when he came to take her for a walk. He seemed relaxed and happy. That was good. Then the very next morning he showed up tense and worried. That was bad. He quickly fed her and hardly petted her at all. He didn't seem to be mad at her, though, just distracted.

"I'll be back after breakfast," he said. "We pulled a special mission." He hesitated, then walked back to the kennel and opened Cracker's gate and laid his forehead on hers. She liked that. She stood as still as she possibly could so she could concentrate on what he was feeling. He was worried. He pulled back. "You remember what a hot zone is, Crack?" He rubbed behind her ears. "They asked for us specifically." He lowered his voice. "It's a secret mission. I don't even know what it is." Manning, Wisconsin, had not prepared Rick for this. His whole future had been laid out for him there. Not many surprises.

Cracker sniffed at his pocket. *Wiener?* Rick pulled it out and heaved her a piece. "Got this from the chef." She gobbled it up. "I don't know how you stay so skinny."

He closed the gate, and she saw him heave a piece of wiener to Bruno. *Hey, that wasn't right . . . oh, well.*

She sat by the gate and waited. He always came back a little while after he fed her. They were probably going to work today. She could tell by how tense he was.

Before Rick returned, she stood up and pushed the tip of her nose through the chain link. She knew he was coming because, well, she just knew. And there he was, with his rucksack on his back. Twenty-Twenty and Cody walked with him. Tristie slapped her paws on the ground and ran to the back of the kennel. Cracker did the same. Then they ran back to the gate and sat their best sit. Rick was almost here! Cracker began hopping in the kennel and pawing the gate.

She was surprised when the other guys walked off in one direction, and Rick heeled her in a different one. She and Tristie looked back at each other before walking off with their guys. Rick seemed nervous, so she felt a little nervous too. She looked up at him as they walked to the helicopter pad and climbed into a chopper. Even though nobody else was on board, Rick looked around anxiously. So Cracker looked around too but didn't see anything unusual.

All Rick knew was that they were headed for Bien Hoa and that the mission involved Special Forces. Special Forces did a lot of secret stuff. Nobody would say exactly what that meant. The Special Forces were basically the roughest, toughest, fastest, smartest, best-trained American soldiers in Vietnam. They were like guys with engineering degrees and black belts at the same time. Superspecialists. In short, nothing like Rick. Rick had actually heard they ate the soles of their own feet when they were starving. *That couldn't possibly be true,* Rick assured himself. *Could it?*

Cracker went to lie in the doorway next to Rick. She loved the windy choppers. Wind was her favorite thing . . . but then so were wieners. She wished Rick had a wiener, but if he did, she would be able to smell it. She glanced at him, but he didn't even glance back. He was frowning.

When the helicopter landed, Rick and Cracker hopped off. Bien Hoa was huge compared to his little camp. He saw another handler with a dog and called out, "Hey, I'm with the 67th IPSD. I'm supposed to go to Special Forces headquarters."

The other guy said, "Hey, I hear you guys have some good dogs." He pointed. "Special Forces is that way."

"Thanks!" Rick said.

He was barely in the building before a man stopped him and said, "Rick Hanski?" Then before Rick could answer, the man said, "I'll go get the Camel." Rick wondered who or what "the Camel" was. He waited with Cracker. He was so nervous, he couldn't tell if he really had to take a leak or if he only thought he had to take a leak. After about twenty minutes a man walked in and straight up to him, holding out his hand for a firm shake.

"I'm Camel. I'll be leading our mission." Camel was broad and didn't look even slightly like a camel. Maybe he smoked them. Camel wore plain O.D. fatigues, no stripes, no dog tags, no distinguishing marks at all. Everything in the army was O.D.–olive drab. A scarf was tied around his neck, and his hands were heavily veined. He reminded Rick of a kid a few years older than him who'd lived on his block.

The kid got in trouble a lot, especially at school, but then he'd gone on to become a cop. Rick remembered something his dad had told him once about being a cop: "It's a thin line. It takes a bad boy to stop the bad boys. The best cops are bad guys who want to do good." Dad the Philosopher. It was weird, though, that line—as thin as a hair, yet it still made all the difference in the world.

Cracker felt alert in all her muscles and her nose and ears and even all the hairs on her body. This man who shook Rick's hand was strong, she could tell, though she figured she could take him if it came to that. She couldn't tell from Rick's response whether this man was Rick's friend or enemy.

"This is Cracker?" the man said.

"Yes, sir."

"Beautiful animal. May I pet her?"

"Of course, sir."

"You don't have to call me sir." Camel softly petted Cracker's head. "Magnificent."

"Yes, sir. She sniffed out a sniper one day. Another day we saw a little action."

"You can call me Camel. You know what I do?"

"Yes, sir, Camel, you're Special Forces. You do . . . stuff we don't know about."

"That's a good description of it."

Rick had to ask. "So why me?"

"Your reputation. Your sergeant said you're the best there is."

"My sergeant?" U-Haul had recommended *him*? Rick felt a jolt of pleasure and shock at the same time. "Thank you, sir—I mean, Camel . . . sir!" Even Rick couldn't help laughing at what an idiot he sounded like. Camel laughed as well.

Camel cocked his head toward the door, and Rick followed, thinking that there'd been a mistake. Could it really be U-Haul who had recommended him? Camel offered a cigarette as they walked outside. *Nice guy!* Rick reached for his lighter, but Camel had paused and was already holding out his. They walked quietly for a bit and then stood under the gray skies smoking. Rick felt like a new kid at school who'd just been befriended by the star of the football team. Camel squinted toward where the sun would be.

"We're going to fly to Tay Ninh to practice for a special mission with your dog."

"What's the mission?" Rick asked. Rick waited.

A split second passed. You wouldn't even have noticed under normal conditions. But Rick could tell Camel was formulating a response instead of speaking spontaneously. "We're executing a rescue. I'm still finalizing the plan."

"You get to make up the plan?"

"Oh, yes. In Special Forces you get the assignment, and then you have to put together a plan."

Rick couldn't help exclaiming, "Cool! We just follow orders." He waited for more, but Camel didn't say anything.

Two men were walking toward them. When the men arrived, one immediately put out his hand. "Vukovich," he said. "You must be Rick and Cracker." Like Camel, the two men wore nothing on their O.D. fatigues to indicate rank or affiliation.

The other man stuck out his hand. "You can call me Madman." Madman spoke so softly, Rick needed to strain to hear him. *Madman?* Rick hesitated nearly imperceptibly before reaching out his hand and saying, "Nice to meet you, Madman."

There was a silence, and Rick got the funny feeling the other three were evaluating him. He tried to stand taller, add an inch to his stature. Then Camel slapped his shoulder. "Let's get going. We got a long day of practice today. We're going to be rescuing some POWs. They're okay, just a few bruises, a little malnutrition, but no broken bones. We're lucky." Rick felt his heart beat faster at the word "rescuing." From where, he wondered.

They walked over to the helicopter pad. The chopper hadn't arrived yet. Madman gently knelt down next to Cracker. Rick said, "Easy, girl," but it wasn't necessary.

Cracker immediately liked this man. He understood her, she could tell. He rubbed her ear. *Oooh, mmmm.* Maybe he could teach this new ear-rubbing method to Rick. *Mmmm.*

Rick felt a stab of jealousy as Cracker seemed almost to be smiling.

Madman stood up. "Very nice dog."

Camel said, "Madman talks to the animals, I kid you not. He's got a master's in psychology, and I swear, sometimes I think he understands every living thing."

Madman actually blushed. Rick asked, "So you work with animals for Special Forces?"

"Nah," said Madman. "I'm a demolitions expert."

Camel laughed, slapped Madman hard on the back. "He blows things up, don't you, Madman?"

Madman just smiled.

The chopper arrived, the noise preventing any further normal conversation.

They all climbed aboard. Camel sure was a nice guy. Rick had never thought much about Special

Forces, but so far they weren't what he expected. He'd assumed they'd act more superior, like they were better than you.

At Tay Ninh they got off and approached the Special Forces compound, a fenced area within the larger base. A sign said CLASSIFIED AREA. Rick hesitated before walking farther. "Camel?"

"Yup."

"I'm just a grunt, man. I don't have clearance."

"We've taken care of all that." Camel kept going, so Rick followed. It dawned on him that if they had clearance for him, they probably knew everything about him. They must have checked him out already, and he hadn't even known it was being done.

Camel, Madman, and Vukovich stopped to talk to a couple of other guys. "Hey, how'd it go?" Camel asked one of them.

The man took on a peculiar expression. "Ah. We found him."

Camel seemed to understand immediately. "I'm sorry," he said, and then Rick got it: The man they were talking about had been found dead.

"Yeah," said the other man.

"Did you talk to his parents?"

"Yeah, yeah." The other man looked away. "Yeah," he said again.

There was a long silence. Vukovich spoke first. "We'd better get started."

The other men walked on.

Camel, Vukovich, and Madman all turned to Rick at the same time. The suddenness of their attention made Rick catch his breath. Then Camel smiled. "Let's have ourselves a good time today. We're going to practice weapons firing, demolition, helicopter insert of the team, movement on the ground, helicopter extraction with STABO rig—a lot of fun stuff. Special Forces uses the STABO for extractions. It's a great harness—never let me down. Cracker's going to love it!" Rick had one overwhelming feeling: He wanted to do good. No. No. He wanted to do great.

The other guys acted as if Rick were one of them. Two Montagnards also practiced with them. Montagnards were the indigenous people of Vietnam, like the American Indians, and they worked closely and loyally with the Special Forces. The "Yards," as Camel affectionately called them, knew the terrain intimately.

So for the rest of the day the six of them fired CAR-15s—a shortened version of the M-16 Rick usually carried—and ran, crept, hid, and jumped. Cracker occasionally sniffed traps that had been set up to test her. Camel had her move faster than she was used to, but she still caught every trap. They also attached the special harnesses Camel had talked about—the STABOs—to themselves and Cracker, and then they were lifted off into the sky as they hung beneath the chopper. Camel had been right. It was just about the most fun day Rick had ever experienced.

As they worked, Rick thought he had never sweated so much in his life. Then, at the end of the day, the other three were suddenly slapping Rick on the back and saying, "Good job." And they petted Cracker and said over and over, "Good dog!" They had a celebratory air about them, and that's when Rick realized that he had *not* been one of them all day, but he was now.

They ate in the mess together that night, not talking about much except sports and dogs and their girls—everything except this damn war. At Camel's insistence, Cracker lay in the mess hall next to them. With Camel doing most of the talking, Rick and the other guys ate the way the guys all ate, basically shoveling food into their mouths in a way Rick's mother would call "bad manners." Rick's mind flitted briefly to home, then back again. "That's the whole point," Camel was saying to Rick. "Six men and a dog, but we're like one creature." But then all of a sudden Rick wanted to know something. "Say, Camel?"

"Yeah?"

"What's the worst thing you've ever seen?"

Camel didn't answer at first. He slowly finished chewing. He swallowed. Then he finally said, "You gotta move on from that kind of stuff. That's the nature of the work, man. You move on from what haunts you. Otherwise, you become like Tommy."

"Who's Tommy?"

Camel paused again, then said, "Lost his nerve. Had to quit." There was a silence while they ate. Then Camel said, almost gently, "Hey, I hear your sister went undergrad to MIT."

Rick said, "Yeah, she's a brain." Then he thought about that. "What, you guys know everything about me?"

Camel smiled. "For some jobs I got higher clearance than the members of Congress. We gotta know who we're dealing with."

They ate quietly, and then the others looked quietly at Camel, as if waiting. Camel seemed kind of pleased, but also displeased. "We did good out there today. But we're going to have to cut the practice short. One day instead of two. We got some new intel, so we don't have time to waste. We got a safe house we'll take you to in the morning." He was talking to Rick.

"Safe house?"

"It's just a house in a village, but it's guarded. We'll be fine."

"So we're starting tomorrow instead of the day after?"

"Yeah. So I want you and Cracker to get a good night's rest."

Rick's heart sped up. A good night's rest? When all this was going on? Later he lay on his cot, Cracker on top of his legs. "My knees, girl," he said, but she didn't budge. He didn't try to push her off, let his mind wander instead. He hadn't goofed here in Vietnam. But he hadn't gone on a killer mission yet. And Cracker, she was the other factor.

He didn't know, because he hadn't asked it of her, whether she was a generalist or a specialist. She'd done everything he'd asked. But now they were stepping up in level. Why him? He could think of two reasons: Bruno had just returned from a kick-butt mission—two weeks in the field. Couldn't over-work the dogs, or they weren't as effective. And Tristie had gotten orders yesterday. So now here he was—the generalist asked to step up, to specialize. But, man, he didn't know. He just didn't know. Did he have the hunger for this kind of stuff? It wasn't too late. He could go to Camel, tell him no. They'd find someone else, lose just a day. But who knows what could happen to those prisoners in a day? He became aware of one of his feet going to sleep and reached down to push Cracker away.

Sometimes Cracker liked to stay right where she was even if he didn't want it. Now, when he reached down and tried to push her off, she stubbornly folded her paws around him. Maybe if he scolded her, she would move.

But Rick suddenly felt too tired even for that. He crashed in mid-thought and woke with his knees aching from Cracker's weight.

After breakfast Camel said, "We'll go in two separate jeeps so the locals don't know what we're up to. Cracker will ride with Madman."

"She won't ride with anyone but me," Rick said confidently. Then he saw Cracker seem to smile as Madman petted her.

Cracker looked from Rick to Madman. She liked this Madman fellow, but Rick was her guy. She sat in front of Rick. Finally, he said, "Go with Madman, Cracker. He's your friend." Madman picked up her leash. Cracker looked up at Rick. "Good girl. Go with Madman." He gave her the "stay" gesture and took a few steps away to stand next to Camel.

Madman said, "Come, Cracker!" She hesitated and looked again at Rick. He didn't know what to do, so he turned his back. When he turned back around, he saw her jumping into the jeep with Madman, Vukovich, and one of the Montagnards. He watched as the jeep drove off, Cracker gazing at him anxiously.

He, Camel, and the second Montagnard waited about half an hour before driving off to the safe house. As described, it was just a hut in a village, with a few Montagnards and Special Forces guys around keeping watch.

Rick was feeling pretty tired. Even his brain felt tired. Camel looked curiously at Rick. "Feel good about going on this mission?"

Rick thought a moment. "Yeah, yeah."

"Good. Listen to your intuition."

Rick blurted out, "I'm a little nervous."

Camel said, "I wouldn't want to go with anyone who wasn't. Sit down, let's all talk."

And there on the floor of that hut, Camel told Rick more mission details while the other men listened and Cracker snored lightly by their side.

Camel smoked cigarette after cigarette as he went

over the plan. "We need to rescue four captured personnel before the NVA takes them up to Hanoi. If they go to Hanoi, we'll never get to them." Camel inhaled and seemed to be waiting for comment from Rick.

Rick concentrated on the new information. "Right. You said 'rescue' earlier," he said. "But you didn't say where from. . . ."

"A jail—more of a pigpen, really. We have coordinates and a picture of the jail from our agent."

Rick was still back on "rescue." He said, "Yeah. Yeah."

"Six of us plus the dog will perform the whole infiltration into the target area."

Oh, man. Rick was slowly getting the picture. And as Rick understood it, "infiltration" meant going into enemy-held territory—and with just six men. His heart raced.

Camel asked sympathetically, "Did you get enough to eat this morning? Need any cigarettes or anything?"

"No, I'm fine." Rick's mouth didn't move right. "Uh. Just so I understand. We're infiltrating enemy-held territory with just six men and a dog?"

"Absolutely." Camel's face was still sympathetic. "We'll get you and your dog out of there, don't worry. We appreciate your help, and we'll take good care of you." He lit a new cigarette from his old one. "Our guys are being held in an enemy camp with five or six guards at all times. Booby traps everywhere. Cracker's going to have a lot to keep her busy." He paused. "But it's all gonna work." Cracker had roused at the sound of her name.

Madman said, "She can handle it. Camel's famous for his intuition." He smiled at Cracker, then slapped Camel's back.

Camel said, "Absolutely, she can."

This was all going a little fast for Rick. He thought, *I ain't famous for* my *intuition*. It didn't take much intuition to sell drill bits. But he took a deep breath, trying to remember how calm his father always was. Rick was a Hanski. Hanskis didn't panic. Still, his heart pounded.

Camel added modestly, "Everybody's got intuition. But, you know, in our line of work, you start to develop it more."

Cracker waited while the men smoked silently. This Camel man was looking at her like he was studying her. She wondered if she was supposed to bite his nose off. She looked at Rick, but he seemed calm. She decided not to bite the man's nose off. The man leaned forward. She growled.

"Easy girl," snapped Rick. "Easy."

She stopped growling.

Rick's mind raced right along with his heart. "But how do you know for sure that the men are there?"

"Our agent told us," Camel said. "Vietcong man. Credible source, though. He's never given us bad intel."

Rick felt his jaw drop but he closed it immediately. He wondered how much he was showing the tumult inside himself. He just didn't see how they could base an entire mission on something Charlie said. He tried to calm down. It was just that he'd heard a thousand times that you can't trust anything the Vietcong said. He couldn't help speaking but tried to make it sound casual. "What if he's a double agent and it's an ambush?"

Cracker was getting agitated. Rick knew that she knew what he was feeling.

Camel laughed wryly. "Oh, yes, we've been ambushed. Oh, yes, that has happened." He chuckled. "But I survived to tell you about it." He pulled something out of his pocket and threw it to Cracker.

Cracker sniffed at the item as it flew through the air. *Food!* She snatched it into her mouth. She decided she liked this new man. But there was something about him. He seemed almost like her. On the other hand, all Rick had to do was tell her to, and she would bite anybody's neck.

Camel silently took a few deep drags, giving Rick a moment to settle down. After a few moments, optimism started to fill Rick. He offered, "Well, practice did go smooth. The plan seems solid."

"It's a good plan," Camel said.

"Do things usually go as planned?" Rick asked. His optimism drained as the other men all laughed.

Madman said, "Remember that time we were surrounded by about two hundred enemy troops and you got pinned down?"

The others laughed more. "That'll be a great story to tell the grandkids!" Camel said.

Rick wanted to say that being surrounded by two hundred enemy troops wasn't a story he'd want to be telling anyone, ever. But he remembered his sister's and his rapt attention as they listened to their grandfather tell about World War II and the Nazis. Hanskis stayed calm. He didn't say more.

There was another brief silence. Then Camel said, "It's a real good plan." More silence. Madman petted Cracker as Camel continued: "The thing about plans is that you can't predict what the enemy is going to do. You can only plan for what you think is going to happen. So when we get out there, you have to try not to ask yourself whether you can do something. Instead, you have to tell yourself, 'I *will* do this.' Not can, but will." He paused, looked up at Rick. "I hear you're a good shot."

"Yeah, I did pretty good in AIT." Shooting well had come pretty easy for Rick. A gun was like some kind of ultimate tool.

Madman nodded approval, but at Cracker. He murmured to her, "Six people and a dog. One creature."

Cracker had no idea what he was saying. But he sure did know how to pet a dog.

They'd planned to spend a short time practicing today just like yesterday, but then as Rick was finishing off a mid-morning snack, Camel rushed in and said, "New intel. Gotta move."

Rick didn't move, and for the first time Camel looked annoyed with him. "Let's move!"

Dammit. Rick had taken some things out of his sack and had to repack them. He was the last one out of the safe house.

Like the other men, Rick was supposed to go on the mission "sterile." That meant no uniform, just plain fatigues. He taped his dog tags together and put them in his pocket. He took off Cracker's metal choke chain so it wouldn't rattle. He pulled

Cracker's STABO harness out of his rucksack and found it all stuck together. He tried to figure that one out. Maybe it had gotten wet somehow and some of the adhesive from the tape had stuck on it? Nah. Maybe . . . He was concentrating so hard, he didn't even notice Vukovich laughing. The other guys started laughing too.

Camel laughed hardest. "Don't worry, that's not her real harness. Vukovich is our glue expert."

Rick wasn't even sure if this was a joke. Maybe Special Forces had some kind of special super-glue? Everyone looked seriously at Rick for a second.

"We're kidding," said Camel.

"Oh!" Rick said. Then he finally got it. Just like every unit had a procurement specialist, it seemed like every one had a practical-joke specialist, too. In this group that would be Vukovich. Rick finally laughed, but by then nobody else was.

They all walked toward a Huey in a nearby field. Rick noticed some of the locals watching them closely. Camel pointed at Vukovich and said, "Hey, when you get off the chopper, don't forget your sack like you did last time!" They both laughed. Rick was shocked at how casual the team seemed.

Cracker had come to accept the others, because now she could feel that Rick felt comfortable with them. When they reached the chopper, Cracker jumped aboard eagerly. They lifted into the sky. Cracker smelled smoke in the air.

"Busy day in Vietnam," shouted Camel.

Rick's feet hung out the doorway. They seemed to be going west, and for a long while. He turned to Camel.

"If we keep going west, we're going to cross the border into Cambodia."

"That's right."

It was illegal under the rules of engagement for the United States to cross the border. Of course, Camel would know that. He would also know that if they got taken prisoner across the border, there was nobody to save them except other Special Forces.

He leaned into Camel's ear and shouted, "The rules of engagement! Won't we get in trouble?"

Camel shouted back, "The president knows about all activity over the border!"

Rick was stunned. The president? Like the president of the United States? Would the president know that he, Rick Hanski, was going over the border?

Sixteen

RICK STARED AT THE JUNGLE BENEATH HIM AND wondered whether they had already crossed into Cambodia. Camel's face was impassive. It was an honor to be chosen to accompany Camel—at least, that's what U-Haul had told him. Rick had mentioned to the sarge that rumor he'd heard about how Special Forces soldiers ate their own soles when they ran out of food. In response U-Haul had basically told him he was so stupid, it was unimaginable that he'd graduated kindergarten. And yet Sarge had recommended him for this gig.

Rick hoped this rescue plan wasn't *dinky dau*. That was supposedly Vietnamese for "nuts." Sometimes a commanding officer came up with a plan that was *dinky dau*. There had been cases Rick had heard of where a unit refused to follow their C.O. if the plan was bad. But these guys seemed to know what they were doing.

They kept going west. Camel hadn't told Rick precisely where they were going, but Rick didn't know much about Cambodia anyway. In fact, he realized he didn't know much about anything. But he finally had to ask. "Where we going?" he shouted out.

"A hamlet called Phumi Krasang in Kampong Province," Camel shouted back.

Rick had never heard of it. The jungle thinned out as the helicopter began to drop down, and Rick's mouth went dry. It was still daylight so the plan, which called for insertion at dusk, was out the window. He tried to lick his mouth moist, but he didn't seem to have any saliva. His heart was pounding so hard that he could literally hear it over the noise of the chopper. He glanced casually at the other guys. They seemed perfectly calm, like they were just flying to the grocery store to buy a gallon of milk.

The chopper didn't touch down, just hovered for a moment. Rick did exactly what they'd done in practice: jump down and rush out with Cracker and take cover behind some bushes. There was jungle but nothing too heavy. More like the woods outside of his town back home. Rick had put on his own and Cracker's STABO harnesses before they got on the helicopter, because everyone had to be ready to extract immediately, just in case something went wrong. In fact, they had to be ready to extract immediately even if everything went right. Rick would be working Cracker off leash for this mission. Rick turned to Camel, who nodded at him. Rick said with quiet urgency, "Search, Cracker."

Cracker padded forward just a few feet before she sat down. It turned out to be some kind of booby trap hung from a tree. They all walked around it in the same order as in practice. First Cracker. Then Rick, one of the Montagnards, Camel, Vukovich, Madman, and the other Yard. At one point Rick waited for Camel and whispered, "Aren't we coming back in this direction? Shouldn't we flag the booby traps somehow? What if a friendly blows them?"

Camel said softly, "We'll remember where they are. Besides, there aren't gonna be any friendlies around here."

Rick wanted to ask, *But how will you remember? It all looks so much the same.* But Camel spoke so confidently that he knew he shouldn't say more.

Cracker alerted to several booby traps within the first twenty yards. Man, this place was loaded. And they were moving fast. Rick studied her so hard that they became a smaller version of six men, one creature. They became dog and man, one creature. She barely had to begin to alert when he knew she had one.

Once when Rick accidentally broke off a twig, he wet a piece of dirt with his saliva and wiped dirt on the broken twig to disguise the fresh break, just like he'd been taught during training. Madman was sanitizing the trail in case any of them missed anything, and the last Yard sometimes walked backward, watching the rear. When night fell, they lay in the bush hardly moving except for when Rick fed Cracker a can of horse meat and the guys ate some dehydrated food mixed with cold water. They'd done all this in practice. Then Rick figured he lay awake for at least three or four hours.

He frowned. Camel, Vukovich, and Madman seemed like three pretty normal guys—stronger and smarter, sure, but were they the supermen who would be needed to pull this thing off?

Rick almost called out in surprise as he heard a leaf fall. But he forced himself to remain silent. He tried to concentrate on the plan:

1. Practice for two days. Instead they'd practiced for one.

2. Take a Huey helicopter to two klicks from the imprisoned men at last light. They hadn't done that. They'd taken the chopper three clicks away not long after first light.
3. Rest for the night.
4. Creep through the woods to the prison at first light.
5. Shoot the guards.
6. Rescue the men.
7. Meet the helicopters that were standing by to pick them all up.
8. Come home as heroes!

Everyone else, even Cracker, seemed to be asleep. But Rick felt like he was sleeping on rocks—he *was* sleeping on a few rocks, as a matter of fact. And he wasn't allowed to take his rucksack off. He needed one arm through it at all times and had to use it like a pillow. Not exactly like his down pillow at home. Not even like the so-called pillow at base. But they had to be ready to move at any time. So he just lay staring at the sky. Clouds hid the stars. Rick tapped a foot before suddenly realizing that the tapping made a soft noise. He tried to stay as still as possible. He was so sleepy, it was almost like he was asleep. Only he wasn't. He turned on his side, but then the sack dug into his ear. Cracker pressed against him, fast asleep.

Rick looked over to where Camel, Vukovich, Madman, and the Yards were lying quietly and wondered if they, too, were awake. Then he wondered what made a man pursue a profession like this. He himself had thought about going to tech college and learning some kind of thing. He just wasn't sure what.

Every man lay within arm's reach of the other. It was so peaceful, Rick could hardly believe what was going down tomorrow. But the team had covered more than half the distance today, and that meant they'd reach their objective early the next morning.

Cracker twitched, and Rick pulled his dog to him and whispered in her ear, "I'll get you out of here, I promise." Then he said forcefully, "I *will* get you out."

Rick didn't think he would ever be able to sleep. Finally, he decided he felt more comfortable on his back. He couldn't remember ever falling asleep on his back in his life. He didn't know why, but it had always been impossible for him to fall asleep on his back. . . . Then it was first light.

Rick was surprised to see the guys just kind of standing around. Shouldn't they get going? Camel seemed to be looking into space, concentrating. Then he turned toward Rick. "Try to get back into the moment," he told him.

Funny, Rick knew exactly what Camel meant. He concentrated, meditated almost, on just being there. His hearing and eyesight grew more acute. It was almost like a supernatural thing. But it was all real. Couldn't put that off any longer. It was real. He was going to whip the world or he wasn't.

They began moving again, even faster than yesterday. Camel had received word that the prisoners were going to be moved to Hanoi that afternoon. Cracker alerted for booby traps time after time, but they still reached their destination pretty much on time. They all crouched in the bush, where Rick saw a hootch that was little more than a pigsty. It was the jail. He watched several Vietcong walk into the pen, and a moment later there was screaming. Rick felt his whole body freeze, but not in a normal way, more like something had taken control of it. He felt a brief fear that he wouldn't be able to move again even if he wanted to. But Camel had warned him about some of the effects of adrenaline, the way it could freeze your body and prevent you from moving. He closed his eyes as tightly as he could for a moment and told himself, *I can move. I will move.* And then he did.

They crept farther back in the bush, and Rick listened as Camel called the forward air controller who would direct the extraction helicopters and also the fast-mover planes that would support them during the mission. *Okay, all according to plan.* Rick felt alert but strangely calm. Camel said softly into his radio, "The hit is going down in thirty minutes."

Then Cracker froze. The hair on her neck stood straight up. Rick turned to tell Camel, but Camel had already noticed. He held up his palm. The other guys already knew whatever it was that was happening. They slipped under cover.

Camel whispered to Rick, "Don't move. Keep your dog still. Don't you or your dog look at their eyes."

"Whose eyes?"

"The V.C. They're right behind us. They can sense it when your eyes are looking at them. Don't look, even if you feel like you have to. Even if you feel like they see you."

Suddenly, it was as if Camel turned into a statue. Rick leaned into Cracker's ear and said, "Easy. Easy, girl."

Cracker lifted her nose into the air and inhaled deeply. She could smell a lot of different people, but the smells were all mixed up together with dirt and gunpowder and moldy leaves and Camel and Rick.

She moved her head slightly and heard Rick hiss, *"Easy."* She froze, except for her nostrils, which kept inhaling. She could feel Camel's foot touching her haunch. She didn't have to look down to know it was Camel's foot and not Rick's. She just knew.

Cracker felt an itch and thought about scratching it. But Rick had said that word—"easy"—with such urgency. She wondered whether "easy" meant "don't scratch." The Camel man didn't move at all. It was weird.

She heard the sound of men moving quietly through the jungle. Her ears rotated, but she couldn't turn them in the right direction without also turning her head. Wasn't it her job to alert Rick to the noise? But he had said, "Easy." Did that mean she shouldn't let him know about the noise? She heard an explosion in the distance and heard a man screaming. She smelled his blood. But she didn't move.

Rick's hold on her was firm, but she could feel a tremor in his hands. There was a small hole in the bush, and she could see men walking by. Rick's hand slid very, very slowly up over her eyes. Then she couldn't see anything but the inside of his hand.

Rick wondered whether a dog's eyes could also alert the enemy. He watched out an opening in the foliage and could see people, not their whole bodies, but just bits of shadow and light. For a while he counted how many shadows passed, but when he got to a dozen, he stopped. Once, one of the shadows stopped, and Rick had a sick feeling that a man was looking right at him. He heard footsteps approaching and quickly lowered his eyes. It was like Camel had said, the man had sensed his eyes. He tried to send a thought to Cracker: *Easy, girl, easy.* She didn't move. Man, she was a great dog. The footsteps paused. Rick felt certain the man could hear his heartbeat. He tried not to let even his lowered eyelids flicker. Dammit, though, he could hear himself breathing. It was quiet, but if he could hear it, maybe they could. The footsteps moved away. They paused again. They moved away again.

Rick became aware of a stick or something digging into his thigh. He wondered what would happen if he shifted slightly. He lifted his eyes and waited. He didn't see any shadows passing. He thought he could shift safely. But he turned his eyes toward Camel, who sat so still, he didn't seem real. In fact, his eyes had taken on an eerie, almost waxy quality. So Rick didn't move either. The feeling of the stick digging into him grew so intense, he almost thought it was worth it to move. But he didn't. He waited. And waited.

Cracker hated staying this still. She obeyed anyway. She felt as if she didn't need to look to know everything that was around her. She could hear a bird in the distance. She could hear a leaf hitting another leaf. She could tell which way the soft breeze was blowing. She could smell that the air was clearing of human smells, except for those of Rick and Camel and their friends. But she ached to move.

For Rick, staying still literally made his body feel as if it were in pain. He wouldn't have thought it was so hard. He watched as his foot involuntarily started to twitch. He thought thirty minutes must have elapsed since the last of the enemy had passed.

Suddenly, Camel's eyes turned unwaxy. Rick heard a waterfall in his ears. It took him a moment to realize that the sound of the waterfall was coming from inside of him, maybe blood rushing through him.

Cracker's hair stood up again, and Rick spotted brush moving. Before he could react, the Yards were shooting. "We're compromised," Vukovich said, surprisingly calmly.

Camel was already on the radio: "The hit is going down."

Cracker noticed that Rick didn't tell her to come. Noise, running, explosions—everything was going on at once. Rick started running, so she ran with him.

She could have run much faster, but she didn't know where they were going. She could feel the urgency in the way they were running. The smells and sounds passed by so quickly, she couldn't really process them the way she'd been taught, but she did smell gunpowder.

Rick did everything the other men did. Basically, they were shooting at anybody who wasn't them. Rick tried shooting at a guard and missed wildly. Then something savage filled him, and he aimed at another guard's head and saw the man's head explode. He was thrown into some kind of savage zone, and he wanted to kill, and he wanted to live. He felt like he was possessed by something, like maybe even the devil, and this thing had taken over his body. Suddenly he was thrown to the ground, watching a man lift a rifle and aim it at him. He thought, *I'm dead.*

Cracker was already airborne by the time the man had lifted his gun.

For Rick, everything went into slow time, clicking instead of flowing like in regular life. He tried to move, but he was going so slowly. So . . . slowly . . . he must be dead. The rifle was inches from his head, but when he tried to move to grab it, it seemed to be miles from his head.

Cracker thumped against the man and heard his gun fire a moment later. She knew just where to sink her teeth: the man's neck. Once his neck was torn, she swung around and saw Rick pushing himself up. He looked in her eyes for just half a second, and she could see he was fine. Then he started running, and she ran after him.

Rick stopped right before Camel and Vukovich tore open the prison door, covered by the others. He saw movement and aimed at a Vietcong; he was back to moving in fast time now. Rick fired and the man dropped. The prisoners emerged running, and he turned and ran with them.

Camel, just ahead of him, shouted into his radio, "Go ahead and launch! We're in contact now. Ready for extraction." Moments later Rick heard the distant whir of choppers in the air. He kept running. He had a weird tunneling feeling, like all he could hear were his own footsteps and the footsteps of the people chasing them. He hoped they were running in the same direction they'd come from so that Camel knew where the booby traps were. Then Rick hardly cared about that. He just didn't want to get caught by whoever was behind them. But he didn't know how much farther he could go. His lungs burned. His thighs burned. His legs didn't have any spring left in them.

Finally, Camel threw out a smoke grenade to
mark their location. Machine-gun fire sounded from
behind—they didn't have much time. A second later
ropes fell through the air. Rick did the thing he'd
insisted on during training. He snapped on
Cracker's harness to the ropes first while Madman
snapped on Camel's. That way, if the chopper
absolutely had to lift, Cracker would be carried up
to safety and Rick would be left to his fate. But
Camel just had time to snap on Rick's harness
before the helicopter raised them into the air. Camel
held them so they wouldn't swing.

Cracker faced forward so that the wind would hit
her full on. Nothing was like this—not driving in a
car with all the windows open, not even riding in a
chopper. This was ecstasy.

The sounds of machine-gun fire moved into the
distance, and Rick looked down to see the woods
they'd just run through. The wind pounded the back
of his head. They roared forward and upward. Rick
figured they must have been three thousand feet
above ground. He clutched Cracker tightly. Camel
glanced at him, a smile on his face. Rick saw three
more Hueys, with a total of eight men dangling. All
alive. Rick grinned.

The helicopters landed at Katum, a Special

Forces camp not far from the border. This was according to plan. *Back to the plan!*

When everybody was on the ground, they all started talking at once. All the prisoners were bruised but in high spirits. He heard Vukovich saying, "And then the dog ripped open the guy's neck," and everybody was petting Cracker and saying, "Amazing dog" and "Good dog" and "What a dog." It was like they all cared more about Cracker than Rick. But he was proud of her too. Madman knelt down and seemed to be murmuring to her. A different helicopter was already waiting to return Rick to Tay Ninh, where another chopper would take him back to his camp.

Camel shook his hand. "You watched our back. You're a good man. I'll make sure to put in a good word for you and Cracker."

Rick got aboard with Cracker and tried to open his rucksack to change Cracker from her harness to her chain. For some reason, the sack was stuck closed. It was as if it were glued shut. Then he laughed.

Seventeen

RICK WOULDN'T HAVE BELIEVED IT, BUT HE FELL asleep on the chopper back to camp. The pilot actually had to shake him awake when they landed. He woke up disoriented and wondered for a second if he'd just dreamed the last few days. But the pilot said, "I hear she's an amazing dog," and he knew it was all true. He and Cracker got off.

Rick and Cracker trudged toward Rick's barrack while men rushed frantically in the opposite direction. One glared at him and shouted, "All available men!" Then U-Haul himself went running past but ran back to say, "Where the hell are you going? All available men."

Rick opened his mouth, closed it, then said, "I

just returned from a special mission." He felt a little, well, important now.

The sarge seemed to be choking on his own saliva as he tried to scream his loudest scream. He looked at Rick as if he were a new breed of worm and screeched, "Is there something about the word 'all' that you don't understand? There are men in trouble out there. Get yourself together and get your tail on a chopper!"

Rick said, "What's going on?"

U-Haul said impatiently, "We got two major battles going on. Lots of casualties. All available men." He dashed off.

Rick couldn't believe that "all available men" meant someone who'd just returned from rescuing four Special Forces soldiers and had barely slept for days. But when he got back to the hootch, every other handler was already gone. He kept thinking about the words "lots of casualties." So he got fresh supplies for himself and Cracker and jogged to the helicopter pad. Only one chopper was left, so he and Cracker jumped aboard.

They neared a field with men lying in the distance. When he and Cracker got off and the chopper left, the silence surprised him. Just the same, he crawled forward rather than walked. He spotted

Uppy in a trench and made his way over to him.

"How's it going?" Rick said.

"They broke the perimeter last night, but we established a new one and it's holding so far. We tried to get everybody available here when the perimeter broke, but there was another big battle going on twenty klicks away."

It was already afternoon by now. "This has been going on since last night?"

"Yeah—the middle of the night."

A gun fired, but just one, then a few fired, then silence again. Then Cracker noticed Tristie at the other end of the trench. A guy she didn't know was holding Tristie's leash. Where was Twenty-Twenty? She tried to pull herself up, but Rick pushed her down.

Rick noticed Tristie too. He readied his gun and peered over the trench and saw Twenty-Twenty lying on his side in the field, almost as if he were sleeping. At first Rick just thought he was entrenched a little farther out, but then he saw blood seeping from Twenty. Rick froze in place and figured it was adrenaline freeze again. But then he realized it was his subconscious comprehending that if he made even one move, the momentum would carry him all the way to where Twenty-Twenty lay, and then they would both end up hurt. But he had to do something.

"Where's the damn backup?" he snapped at Uppy. "My buddy's out there!"

"It's too hot to get him now," Uppy answered, snapping his gum.

Rick suddenly felt like grabbing that gum out of Uppy's mouth and stuffing it up his nose. Instead, he tried to stay calm. He said, as if Uppy were an idiot, "But it's quiet now."

Uppy answered, "My best friend's out there too. We've known each other since second grade. You know?"

Rick took in a breath. "I'm sorry, man. I didn't mean nothing. I . . ."

"Forget it."

Then Twenty-Twenty lifted his head to look up, and a shot rang out. But it wasn't at Twenty-Twenty, it was at Rick, for sticking his head out of the trench. Savageness rose in Rick again. He wanted to blast every Vietcong in the world to smithereens.

Tristie started barking. Somehow she'd gotten off leash and was leaping into the air. Twenty-Twenty screamed, "No, Tristie, stay. Stay!"

Cracker yelped. Rick shouted, "Cracker, stay! Somebody grab that dog! Tristie, stay!"

A soldier lunged at Tristie. But she was too quick. She lurched off. In mid-leap a single shot rang out.

Blood splattered in every direction, and Trisitie fell like a stone, half in and half out of the trench. Rick and Cracker crawled frantically toward her as a soldier pulled her back in.

Something about the triumph of the Special Forces mission mixed with the horror of seeing blood spurting from Tristie made Rick think he might be losing his mind. He cried out to nobody in particular, *"What the HELL is going on?"*

The force of his cry startled Cracker. She'd never heard anything like it from him, and maybe nothing like it from anyone, ever. She'd heard cries of physical pain. But this was a different kind of pain, and also a different kind of Rick. She sniffed at Tristie: alive. She looked at Rick to tell him to do something. People could do things.

Rick could hear Twenty-Twenty crying out, "Is she alive? Is she alive?"

The blood from Tristie's limp body oozed from her chest. She wasn't moving. Rick held her muzzle shut and blew air into her nostrils. She came back to life, whinnying like a horse. Rick blew more air into her nostrils, then hollered, "Medic!"

Uppy said, "The medic's got a pile of humans he's working on." But then Uppy tore off his shirt and pressed it against the wound.

Rick continued blowing into Tristie's nostrils.

Then she opened her eyes and looked right at him before closing her eyes and ceasing to breathe again. "Come on, Tristie!" He kept blowing, but she fell limp, and he knew she was gone.

Cracker also knew she was gone.

"Hey, Rick!" It was Twenty.

Rick didn't answer at first, because he knew what the next question would be. But then he ended up hesitating so long that he realized Twenty already knew what the answer was. Twenty-Twenty didn't speak again.

Rick gently set down Tristie's head and turned away and didn't move for a long time.

Cracker laid her body over Tristie's but kept a paw on Rick. She knew she couldn't protect Tristie anymore, but she still felt protective. When a soldier moved nearby, she snarled and the soldier moved back. Tristie smelled muddy and bloody and just like Tristie, except dead. Cracker had smelled rats and birds right after they died, and they smelled different in death. After Tristie had smelled different for a while, Cracker knew it was time to take care of Rick again. She pushed against him. She couldn't feel anything coming from him, like sadness or anything. That made her feel worried.

The hot sun slanted from the sky and eventually descended as Cracker panted from the heat. Gunfire occasionally broke the peace. When evening fell, the trees loomed dark and large. Several times Rick thought he saw movement in the forest and raised his rifle. But it turned out to be a shadow. Rick squeezed Cracker to him and waited. A long time ago one of Rick's uncles had taken him through the Mojave Desert in southern California. Weird-shaped trees called Joshuas filled the desert, their limbs bent, seemingly misshapen. Crazy, humanlike shapes. His uncle had told him that Joshua trees looked human because they once had been, in another life. He said the trees were ghosts and that each had a story to tell. Rick figured that after tonight these trees by the battlefield would have some stories.

Finally, mortar fire exploded in the distance. Several guys shouted for joy, and Rick realized he was one of the guys shouting. Illumination flares, hanging on parachutes, floated down, imbuing the sky with an eerie daylight and moving shadows across the jungle. The lights slowly floated to the ground, making the whole world seem inside out. It was as if everything inanimate came to life, and everything alive was ghostly. Rick didn't know whether the ache in his gut was real or psychological, or whether it made a difference which it was.

For a long time not a single shot broke the silence. The medic moved into the field to Twenty-Twenty, and then the doc and another guy carried him to an area with other wounded. Rick went to talk to him, but the doc had started an I.V. and Twenty must have gotten a shot of morphine, because he didn't seem to recognize Rick.

Rick didn't sleep, or maybe he did. Sometimes in Nam you couldn't tell. At one point when he was definitely awake, the clarity of the stars startled him. The moon had risen over the nipa palms at the edge of the jungle. Smoke from the battle crept like mold through the air. He dozed fitfully, and when the sun rose, the smoke had cleared. Men moved about. Rick was damn glad to see that all the men were friendlies.

Cracker looked at him expectantly, and he realized he hadn't even fed her or given her water before he fell asleep. *Damn.* She'd saved his life on the Special Forces mission, and he hadn't even remembered to feed and water her. He did both now, then pushed himself up.

She started to follow him but stopped to sniff at Tristie, only Tristie wasn't there anymore. That is, her body was there, but she wasn't. Cracker whimpered and lay down next to Tristie. She pawed again at Tristie like she always did when she wanted to play with her friend.

"Come, Cracker."

Cracker obeyed, but more reluctantly than usual. She wanted Tristie with them. But she had to follow Rick. They kept walking until they reached Twenty-Twenty, lying among the wounded. Blood-smell filled the air.

The unit must have run out of stretchers, because some of the wounded lay on ponchos. Twenty-Twenty had a poncho both over and under him. Even though his eyes were closed, he still wore his glasses. He didn't seem to be breathing. Rick's own breath caught. He braced himself and squatted down, then took his friend's hand and knelt with his forehead on the hand.

"What the hell are you doing? I ain't dead yet," Twenty-Twenty said.

Rick dropped his hand and scurried to his feet as if Twenty had come back from the dead. His friend tried to push himself to a sitting position. "Lie down!" Rick said.

"She's gone, isn't she?" His eyes seemed to be blurry.

"Just lie down, man."

But Twenty-Twenty pushed onto his uninjured elbow and spotted his dog, her fur matted with blood. He collapsed backward. "I told her to stay," he said angrily. Rick wasn't sure whom he was angry at.

"I heard you. We all heard you."

"I *told* her to stay!" The intensity of Twenty's anger was palpable. Rick wanted to say, *But she was only trying to help, don't be angry at her,* but then he decided to leave it alone.

"She didn't stay," Twenty-Twenty said. "I didn't teach her right." Then Rick realized Twenty was angry with himself.

"She was a good dog. You taught her great."

"I'm going back to the world, aren't I?" "The world" was what guys called the real world, America.

Rick barely glanced toward Twenty-Twenty's injured arm, but the glance was enough. "Yeah, you're going back home."

"With how many arms? I don't wanna look. Pick up the poncho."

"You're gonna be okay" was all Rick could say. He wanted to look over at Twenty's wound again, but he already knew. Worse: worse than a Million Dollar Injury. Basically, from the way the poncho lay, it looked like maybe most of Twenty's arm could be gone.

"You make sure Tristie gets buried properly. Make sure, Rick, okay?"

"I will." At the firebase the old-timer dog handlers had already set up a graveyard for the dogs who got killed in action or died of jungle diseases.

"I want her epitath to say 'Sleep well.'"

"All right."

"I'd already decided, just in case."

"Yeah, okay."

"And cut off a piece of my hair and bury it with her."

Rick took out the knife all soldiers carried and cut off a chunk of Twenty's hair. He stuffed it in his pocket.

Rick looked out into the field. He couldn't believe what he saw in the distance: dead bodies, lots of them, beyond the perimeter. Dozens upon dozens of dead V.C. Did that mean they had won the battle? It didn't feel like they had won.

Cracker sniffed at Twenty-Twenty's arm. Blood. She lay down, her head resting on her paws, while the medic leaned over to check Twenty-Twenty. Then she followed while Rick and the medic carried Twenty-Twenty's stretcher and laid him next to a group of other men on stretchers, other men who smelled like blood and guts and dirt. But they were alive.

"What's going on?" asked Twenty-Twenty.

"You're goin' home, buddy. The medevac will be here soon. You'll be fine. There's guys a lot worse off than you."

Twenty-Twenty turned his head away suddenly, crying. "She wouldn't listen," he said one last time. "It's my fault."

Rick said, "It ain't your fault." He looked around. "I think they want to look you over again. You call me if you need anything." But Twenty-Twenty didn't answer.

A man who was clearly badly wounded lay unattended. He looked as if he were made of mud. Rick hesitated, then asked someone, "Shouldn't the medic be looking over that guy?"

"It's triage, man," the other soldier said softly.

"His eyes are open."

"Yeah, but Doc has to work on the guys he can save. That one's a goner."

Rick looked again. The "mud man" seemed alert, bizarrely hyper. A poncho covered most of his body. Whatever made the medic determine the guy was a goner was hidden under that poncho. Obviously, it was more than a lost limb. Rick walked over. The sun made the man's brown eyes hold a glimmer of gold in them. The eyes blinked at Rick. Rick reached for his hand and pressed it. It felt cold.

"Need anything, soldier?" He didn't even know the guy's name. As a matter of fact, he probably didn't know the names of 90 percent of the guys here.

The guy shook his head. He was staring at something. Rick turned to look. It was a bloody thing . . . a foot lying on the ground. The guy said, "Is that mine?" His feet stuck out from underneath the poncho covering his torso.

"No, you got your legs," Rick assured him. "Your feet, too." He hesitated, then lied, "You're gonna be okay. Dust-off's coming." Just as he said it, he heard the choppers in the air. He lied again: "There are guys worse off than you. So you may not be first."

"That's okay, take them first."

Rick lit a cigarette and offered it to the soldier. The soldier opened his mouth slightly, and Rick placed the cigarette in between the poor guy's lips. He inhaled deeply.

Cracker sniffed at the man, which made him smile, cracks breaking the mud on his face. Rick smiled too.

"Nice dog," the man said.

"Yeah, she's great."

"I got an Australian shepherd back home. They're sheepherders." He smiled again.

Then the man shuddered. The life drained from his face, the way light drains from the sky at sunset. But it was weird how the sun still glowed off his eyes. Rick hoped his last thought had been of his sheepherder back home. Rick adjusted the poncho where it had fallen loose.

He walked away, lay down in the grass, and just stared at the sky as two dust-offs arrived to gather the first batch of wounded. Usually the guys would have cheered at the sound, but everybody was so wasted that nobody made a sound. Twenty-Twenty remained, but a medic was looking him over. That made Rick feel a little better—if Twenty's arm were really bad, he'd be the first to go. Probably.

Then Cracker actually got up and left him, trotting over to sniff at Tristie before turning to Rick. "Woof!" He walked over and picked up Tristie, unsure where they should wait.

It was odd the way Rick didn't feel anything. It wasn't as if his heart and mind were back home or with his buddies or his family or anywhere at all. It was as if all his feelings were simply gone, *pfft*. No feelings at all. Not for Twenty-Twenty, not for the dead soldier, not for the dead dog in his arms.

He sat down with Cracker and Tristie far away from everybody else. He remembered that not long after the sarge had first suggested he change dogs, he had gone to sit behind a warehouse. His friends had noticed he'd been gone awhile and started calling his name. "Rick! Rick!" But he didn't answer. He'd just sat there, not really even thinking about much. He felt kind of that way now: *Leave me alone, world.*

So he just stared straight ahead, numb. Then, suddenly, he felt and thought everything he hadn't felt just a few minutes earlier. He was so damned glad that he and Cracker were alive. He thought about his mission with Camel. And he thought about Tristie, Twenty-Twenty, the dead soldier with the sheepherder back home, and how it all sucked. It really, really sucked. But he also had another crazy feeling. It all sucked, but it was just so damn real. And the fact that it was so damn real made it suck more, but it also made it suck less. 'Cause this was *it*. This was the biggest stuff that was ever going to happen in his life. And he'd done good. Whether it was generalist or specialist or applying himself or none of the above, who knew? All he knew, and he *knew* it, was that he'd done good.

He felt as if his cells physically craved something but that the only way to satisfy them was not to get something, but rather to sob, which he did. He couldn't even remember the last time he'd sobbed. He thought all the way back to first grade and couldn't remember sobbing. Oh, he'd shed a tear here and there, but full-on sobbing? Never that he could remember.

He lay down again and waited for the next wave of choppers that would be coming soon to take them back to base.

Cracker moved her snout to his chest. Rick smiled and stroked her long ears. That felt nice, and she could tell it made him feel better. Her ears perked up: more choppers. She stood, and sure enough, in a moment the sky filled with the sound of metal birds. This time the men cheered. Rick seemed invigorated, which in turn made Cracker feel invigorated.

There were only three choppers. The first dropped off supplies and carried away another batch of wounded men.

Rick set Tristie near his rucksack and walked over to the supply drop to grab a couple of canteens of water. He had food in his sack, but he hadn't brought enough water.

Cracker followed Rick as he walked away and stopped to pour water into his steel pot. She gulped it down. He drank the rest of a canteen in one go. Then Rick looked over the dead field. It looked like nothing would grow there again for a thousand years.

"Rick!"

Rick rushed over to where Twenty-Twenty was just about to be lifted into a dust-off. "What is it?" The chopper blades blasted their hair and uniforms with air.

Twenty-Twenty shouted above the noise, "Make sure about Tristie. Don't leave her in the field."

"You got my word. I'll be contacting you. Take care, buddy."

"Yeah, you too." He weakly reached out his good hand, and Rick shook it. "If I don't make it—"

"You're gonna make it."

"—tell my mom I . . . just tell her the truth. Tell her what it was like. She'd want to know that."

"You're gonna make it, man. Quit whinin'! You're going home. You got a Million-Dollar Injury." Rick let his eyes fall just briefly on where Twenty's arm should be.

"I still haven't looked under the poncho," said Twenty-Twenty.

"The doc'll take good care of you."

"You think? You think he'll save my arm?"

It seemed like the injured men were obsessed with their limbs. Rick didn't want to out-and-out lie to his friend. So he said, "They got great doctors. I heard one of them was doing his residency at Yale when he got the letter to serve. They ain't slackers." "You're gonna be lying on the beach in a few months. Send me a picture from Florida. I'll be just about to DEROS while you're running around with your girlfriend."

Twenty-Twenty closed his eyes as a couple of men carried him off. Rick could hear Twenty-Twenty shouting to one of the guys carrying him, "For all intensive purposes, these choppers take you to your death, and then they save your life."

Rick walked with Cracker back to where Tristie lay with her chest caved in. At least it had been fairly fast. He thought maybe he shouldn't have given her mouth-to-mouth. Maybe it had just prolonged her suffering. Maybe it was one of those cases where you did the right thing at the wrong time. No. No, he would have done the same for Cracker. If there had been even the slightest chance to save Cracker, he would have tried. He leaned on his pack and waited for the chopper that would take them back.

Cracker sniffed at Tristie again. She knew Tristie

was gone, but she pawed at her to come back. She pawed at Rick to bring Tristie back. But they both just lay there. She whined but finally lay down.

Chopper after chopper arrived, and soon there were just a few men left. Rick had to go last because he had dogs and because he wasn't injured. The army had priorities. Hurt men. Well men. Dead men. Well dogs. Hurt dogs. Dead dogs. Soon no one else was left, and Rick got ready to climb on board the last chopper. The pilot shouted out, "Sorry, we're overloaded as it is. No room for the dogs."

"Two dogs ain't gonna make a difference," said Rick. "The dead one weighed only fifty *before* she lost blood."

"Can't risk all these human lives for a dog, dead or alive."

Rick just stood there. "All right, can you take the live one and I'll stay behind?"

"Sure. We'll send another bird right out."

"Go on, Cracker, get on the chopper." But Cracker wouldn't budge. He picked her up and threw her on. She jumped right off. He tried again. Same result. "Get on the chopper!" he screamed at her. She pressed against his legs. "All right, stay with me, you crazy dog."

Rick watched the whirring blades move into the

distance. He heard a gunshot from behind him, and he fell to the long grass to hide. "Down!" he cried out to Cracker. She obeyed immediately. But he didn't hear anything more. Still, he didn't move. He kept thinking of the way Camel had become a statue. He lay like a fallen statue, the tall grass wavering around him.

He knew Charlie would come out to police up any ammo or food the G.I.s had left behind. As he listened for every small sound that might mean the enemy was near, he didn't and couldn't understand what he was doing here in Vietnam. And then he had a flicker of realization. The flicker grew stronger. He was here to be doing exactly what he was doing: taking his friend's dog to a proper burial. That meant more to him right now than whipping the world.

His body involuntarily shuddered as he saw Cracker's ears go up in alert. For a moment he thought they were both about to die. He breathed very slowly through his nose, not his mouth, so as not to stir even the air around him. Then he heard it: the *whomp-whomp-whomp* of the chopper blades. He shouted for joy.

Eighteen

THE CHOPPER HAD COME JUST FOR THEM. THE PILOT
looked curiously at them as they climbed aboard.
"Did you really stay just for the dogs?" the pilot
called out over the sound of whirring blades.

"Yeah!" Rick called back. "Thanks for coming."

"It's my job."

Rick laid Tristie down, then set his gun and rucksack beside her. Down below he saw something he
hadn't seen before: leafless trees where American
defoliants had killed off the forests. Spooky.

He looked at Tristie. If someone had told him a
couple of years ago that he would risk his life for a
dead dog, he would have laughed. He lay back. He
felt weird in his chest, like his fatigue was not just in
his muscles and brains, but even in his internal

organs. It was as if even his lungs were exhausted and needed rest. He had the shakes but wasn't sure if that was because of the vibrating helicopter. He didn't usually feel like this in a chopper.

Cracker felt worried. Rick seemed unhappy, and her pal Tristie was dead. She sniffed at Tristie. She knew where Tristie had gone. It was to another place. Once, Willie had owned a fish, and it went to another place too. Of course, that was because Cracker had knocked it out of the water with her paw. . . . Anyway, Tristie would be okay in the other place, but it made Cracker sad that she was gone. She vaguely remembered walking down the aisles of a dog pound back in Chicago among all those doomed dogs. Some of them jumped wildly up and down, yelping to be saved, but many were so depressed, they just lay at the back of their cages and didn't move. She wondered why Willie had taken her there. The way those depressed dogs had lain in their cages, not caring whether they stayed in this place or went to the next place—that was the way Rick seemed now. He seemed like he just didn't want to move or think or feel or do anything at all. He seemed like he didn't care if he was alive. She stood on top of him and looked straight down at his eyes, touching her long nose to his short one.

He smelled strong today. She whacked his chest.

"Owww," he said, but he smiled, so she whacked his chest again. "Ow, you crazy dog." Then he sat up and hugged her hard around her neck. "You crazy dog. You crazy dog."

Even Willie had never hugged her like this before, so desperately. It was as if she were saving his life or something, just by letting him hug her. She stood very still and let his hug sink in throughout her body. He rubbed his head on her head. She kept staying very still. He seemed to like that, and staying still helped her feel his hug better. She was disappointed when he let go of her.

They sat looking out the doorway together at the green, overgrown world below. When the chopper landed, she jumped out and waited while Rick threw down his sack, picked up Tristie, and climbed out. Rick thanked the pilot, who promptly took off, maybe to another battle and more dead and wounded.

Cody hurried over to him. "I was waiting. I heard what happened. I was on another mission, but we got back a few hours ago." He ran his hand over Tristie's head.

Tristie's body felt odd in Rick's arms. She didn't even feel like a stuffed animal. She felt like she was made of wood, and her body was curled into an unnatural position, her chin seemingly glued to her chest. Cracker paced back and forth, occasionally stopping to touch noses with Bruno, who sat somberly watching.

"She was safe in a trench but wanted to go to Twenty-Twenty," said Rick. A cloud broke and rain began flooding from the sky. And it was supposed to be the dry season.

Cody said, "Let's do it." They glanced at the sky; but if this had to happen in the pouring rain, then it had to happen in the pouring rain.

Cracker followed them to the place where all the dead dogs were. She lay in the mud with Bruno while Rick and Cody shoveled a hole. She knew exactly what the hole was for. She'd seen other men digging holes here, but this was the first time the hole was for a dog she liked. She felt kind of surprised when the loud man came and began digging with Rick and Cody. The loud man didn't make a sound.

Once, when the men took a rest, she started digging in the hole. For some reason, that attracted a crowd. A lot of the guys in camp came to watch in their ponchos while she furiously scratched her claws into the wet dirt. Mud flew everywhere. A couple of cameras clicked in the rain.

Finally, Rick called her off, and she stood to the side and watched them dig more. Rick felt it again, the thing he'd felt out in the field earlier—the sense of being at the center of the universe, exactly where he should be, doing exactly what he should be doing. He and Cody gently picked up Tristie and lowered her into the hole. Everything was so slippery, they ended up dropping her down a little harder than they'd expected. Rick winced. Then he reached into his pocket and dropped in Twenty's hair.

They covered up the hole, and that was the last Cracker saw of Tristie. She could still smell her, even in the rain and beneath the mud, but she knew she wouldn't see her again. She lay down on the grave.

Cody turned to Rick, "What should we write on the sign?" Each of the graves had a sign posted on it.

"Twenty said he wanted it to say 'Sleep well.'" He looked over the graveyard: THE KING. RUFUS, ALL-AMERICAN BOY. REBEL, FASTEST DOG EVER. He looked at Cracker and felt a fierce determination rise in him. She would never die, he would make sure of it. He wouldn't even think of what he might write on her gravestone, because she wasn't going to have one.

One of the guys who had good handwriting made the sign for them, and another guy with a camera took a couple of pictures to send to Twenty. Cody and Rick and a few other handlers smoked cigarettes together as the rain relented. Even Sarge smoked quietly. Then Sarge said, "Rest in peace. You were a great dog, Tristie."

Rick was suddenly desperate for a shower. He felt like if he could just shower, he could get rid of some of the memory of today. He kenneled Cracker and showered. Man, it felt better than any shower he'd ever taken.

Afterward he washed Cracker and read his mail. He wasn't surprised to find another letter today from the kid Willie. That kid was stubborn like nothing Rick had ever seen. But Rick still had never gotten around to writing him. What could Rick say to a kid about war that wouldn't be glossing over the whole thing? Rick didn't even sit down as he read the letter. It was just about the same thing every time:

Dear Soldier,

Hi. I am Cracker's owner, or former owner. Since I'm only twelve, I guess my parents were the official owners, but she was really my dog. She was my best friend. Cracker likes wieners, walks, petting, and lying around. She also likes the beach and boats. I know I keep telling you a lot of the same stuff, but since I haven't heard from you, I know you're not getting my letters.

I took Cracker on a boat once. The only
thing about her is that you can't keep feeding
her even if she begs you because she will
never stop eating if you let her. Will you write
me back and send me a picture? I am sure
Cracker is doing really well because she is
really smart. I taught her ninety words. Okay,
sometimes she forgot a word, but she remembered
most of them. She didn't always listen real
well, so I hope you taught her to listen so she
doesn't get hurt. Maybe someday Cracker will
be my dog again. What do you think? Meanwhile,
you take care of her.
    Yours truly,
    Willie Stetson
P.S. Cracker likes to watch baseball games
with me. I am a Cubs fan.

Just about the same letter, over and over.
Obsessive kid, not stubborn. Rick tried to remember
himself at twelve. He smiled. He remembered feeling surprised way back then when someone called
him a "kid." A "kid" was seven, *maybe* eight. But not
twelve. Rick couldn't imagine Cracker being someone else's dog. Cracker was *his* dog. He threw the letter to the side, then took a big breath and picked it

back up. *All right already.* He'd write the kid. But then he put it off, unsure what he wanted to say.

Cody was lying on his cot reading his mail. He got about five times more mail than anyone else in the squad.

"Hey, Cody."

"Yeah."

"You know what we should do?"

"What?"

"Sign up for a second tour of duty. Then we could stay with our dogs."

Cody looked sad. "Already thought about it. But this whole Vietnamization thing Nixon is doing—the North and South Vietnamese are gonna take over the war among themselves while the Americans pull out."

"I thought maybe that was just a rumor."

"I heard it's for real."

Rick lay back and thought that over. "Hey, did you hear the rumor about that guy who got a vet to knock out his dog and then stuck him in his duffel bag?"

"Yeah. Do you think that's true?"

"I don't know. It's possible. Like if you had a friend working customs or something."

But Rick knew in his heart that it wasn't possible. No way could you sneak a dog as big as Cracker home. Besides, he didn't have any friends in customs.

He glanced at Willie's latest letter. Maybe stubborn wasn't so bad. Neither was obsessive. So he got some army-issue stationery and sat on his bunk with Cracker at his side.

DEAR WILLIE,

    SORRY I DIDN'T WRITE YOU SOONER. I'M NOT MUCH OF A WRITER. CRACKER IS DOING GREAT. I THINK SHE'S THE BEST DOG IN VIETNAM. SHE'S NEVER MISSED A BOOBY TRAP. WE WENT ON ONE MISSION WHEN SOMEONE PUT IN A SPECIAL REQUEST FOR OUR TEAM BECAUSE OF HER REPUTATION.

Rick chewed on the end of his pen and thought before writing more.

    I FEEL LIKE I KNOW HER BETTER THAN I HAVE EVER KNOWN ANYONE IN MY LIFE. YOU RAISED A GOOD DOG. YOU DID GOOD. SHE'S SAVED A LOT OF LIVES.

    JUST CURIOUS—DO YOU KNOW ANY SENATORS OR IMPORTANT PEOPLE WHO MIGHT PUT IN A GOOD WORD FOR HER? JUST ASKING, EVERYTHING'S FINE. JUST ASKING. GOOD LUCK WITH THE CUBS. I'M A FOOTBALL MAN MYSELF.

Wisconsin had a baseball team—the Milwaukee Brewers—but they'd just moved from Seattle, and Rick wasn't much of a fan.

Then he decided to write another letter, this time to Twenty-Twenty's uncle, the famous lieutenant colonel.

DEAR LIEUTENANT COLONEL BUTLER,

I AM A MEMBER OF THE 67TH INFANTRY PLATOON (SCOUT DOG). YOUR NEPHEW ORRIN "TWENTY-TWENTY" BUTLER IS A PAL OF MINE. IT HAS BEEN A PRIVILEGE TO SERVE WITH HIM. AS YOU PROBABLY WILL HAVE HEARD BEFORE YOU RECEIVE THIS LETTER, TWENTY-TWENTY WAS INJURED TODAY AND WILL PROBABLY BE SENT HOME. UNFORTUNATELY, HIS DOG TRISTIE WAS KILLED AS SHE TRIED TO GO TO HIM IN THE FIELD. MY PAL CODY AND I BURIED TRISTIE FOR HIM.

THIS MAY BE OUT OF LINE TO ASK, BUT WHEN I DEROS AT THE END OF MY TOUR, I'M WONDERING IF YOU KNOW WHAT WILL BECOME OF MY DOG, CRACKER. SHE HAS SAVED A LOT OF LIVES, AND I FEEL SHE DESERVES A BETTER LIFE THAN DYING HERE IN VIETNAM SOMEDAY. I WAS WONDERING

WHETHER YOU COULD HELP ME WITH THAT?
AS TWENTY-TWENTY WILL TELL YOU, SHE WAS
GREAT BUDDIES WITH TRISTIE.
RESPECTFULLY,
PRIVATE RICHARD CARVER HANSKI

It was hard work writing to a lieutenant colonel. Rick had to look up a couple of words in a dictionary to make sure he hadn't made any mistakes. Sounded crazy, but he'd never realized how useful a dictionary could be.

When he finished, he went outside, wondering where Cracker had gone. Usually when he didn't kennel her, she just lay next to him by his cot. He found her, lying on Tristie's grave, sleeping. She was probably as tired as he was. But he was the kind of tired where although his head felt like it was full of dust and his body ached, his mind raced so wildly that he didn't think he could sleep. His mind ping-ponged around everything that had happened over the last couple of days. He'd killed a man, shot another, and he couldn't regret it. He'd seen his friend wounded and Tristie die. He'd watched a fellow soldier take his last breath.

Cracker was so tired, she didn't even wake up when he walked off. When he returned with food and water for her, she was still lying on the grave. He sat next to her, and she opened her eyes. She ate and drank halfheartedly. Though he'd just bathed her, dirt already covered her nails. Her paw pads were cracked. He'd give her another bath as soon as he got the energy, but at the moment he felt like he'd never have energy again.

"Come on, girl, let's sit somewhere else." He got his poncho and they stretched out far away from the dog graveyard. He realized he'd already missed mess hall. He was starving, but for some reason, that felt good. It was like penance—why did one man die and not another? He stared at the horizon.

He remembered staring at another horizon when he was a boy. He was visiting his maternal grandparents one winter and sitting on a lawn chair watching the northern lights. Back then anything had seemed possible.

The next few weeks were pretty quiet, except Cody started to drive everyone nuts when he decided that Twenty-Twenty was right all along and that those eye exercises really did work. At least Twenty would do them off on his own, but Cody would start rolling his eyes right while he was talking to you. He'd be talking about one of his obsessions—mostly food—and suddenly his eyes would dart to the left and up and around. He swore his eyes were already getting better.

One morning Rick and Cracker pulled another routine mission: clearing a village. It was a one-day mission, because it was Thanksgiving and the mess hall would be serving turkey to the men for dinner that night. The "Donut Dollies"—what they called the girls who worked as American Red Cross volunteers— would be doing the serving. All the guys were look- ing forward to it. American girls. Girls who could speak English.

Rick and Cracker had cleared villages several times before.

The unit Rick was supporting today took APCs— armored personnel carriers—to just outside a village to check for the enemy. This approach was a little irrational in Rick's opinion, not that anybody cared about his opinion. APCs made so much noise that any Vietcong hiding out in the village would be long gone. The whole thing was so irrational, in fact, that some of the other assigned guys actually spoke of refusing to go. Rick had heard about some units that refused to follow orders, but this was the first time he'd heard such talk in person. In the end, every- body climbed aboard.

Rick felt like he was suffocating inside the APC. It was his first time inside one. But he didn't expect to see any action. There were lookouts all over the place. The Vietcong had lookouts and the ARVN had lookouts and the NVA had lookouts, and they all looked like peasants to Rick. He'd heard that sometimes the lookout could be a twelve-year-old girl and she might signal Charlie by doing something as simple as putting her hair behind her ear. Then Charlie would hide or move on.

A few hours into the mission the APCs stopped for some reason. The lieutenant called out, "Just heard over the radio: They're going to bring lunch before we clear the village. Today's your day, gentlemen. The Donut Dollies are coming out here on choppers just to feed us."

The men cheered. They all threw down their sacks and sat in the sun in a nearby LZ, or landing zone, waiting for the girls. As usual, a lot of guys came over to pet Cracker.

"I got a Doberman at home," one told Rick. "What do you have?"

Rick said a little sheepishly, "I don't have a dog."

"Really? How'd you end up a handler?"

He didn't want to say he'd gone begging to a friend of a friend, so he said, "I had a knack for it." The guy seemed to accept that.

The sun felt good on Rick's face. Everything felt

pretty good at the moment. All the men were happy, the sky was clear, and—most importantly—girls were on the way.

There was one Donut Dolly in particular they were all after. And she knew it too. Rick hated girls like that.

"I hope Caroline serves me," said one guy.

Rick didn't even know the guy's name, but he replied anyway. "She's a snob. I like a more down-home girl."

"She may be a snob, but she's a foxy snob."

One guy had brought a radio, and they all quieted as "Hey, Jude" played on the army station. Then they all started singing, even when the song reached the part where the only lyrics were, *Nah. Nah. Nah. Nah-nah-nah-nah.* Cracker wandered around getting petted by all the men. Rick watched her proudly. This was shaping up to be a fairly acceptable Thanksgiving.

When the choppers started roaring, all the men jumped up. Rick tried to get a glimpse of Caroline's long hair. Not that he cared about the snotty princess, but he couldn't help looking. There were only two choppers, but there were probably girls and food on both of them. *There!* He thought he spotted Caroline's hair. But the choppers just hovered low above the LZ, and a couple of burly guys pushed big boxes out the door. Then the choppers roared off.

For a second Rick tried to comprehend. Unless the girls were crammed into those boxes, there were no girls. Someone tore open a box, which was filled with smaller boxes, which were filled with turkey, mashed potatoes, and stuffing. All the guys were crying out, "Where are the girls?" The commander said he didn't know. The radioman was calling into base and reported that the Red Cross had decided the girls should stay put because there had been a report of Charlie in the area. One man complained, "There are *always* reports of Charlie in the area. We're in Vietnam, man."

The men ate sullenly before climbing back into the APCs.

Cracker didn't like the APC. It was noisy and all she could smell was gasoline. The smell filled her nostrils and she couldn't get it out.

The APCs tore through the jungle for another couple of hours—according to the lieutenant, they were going to a different village than planned. Who knew why? The guys hardly seemed to care. Rick just leaned back and accepted his fate.

Rick rarely worked with Cracker on a leash anymore, but when they got out, he attached her so she wouldn't chase any chickens or other animals. He looked around. The village was typical—just a hamlet, really—maybe twenty-five thatched huts surrounded by rice paddies. Jungle in the distance, an ox or two. Rick didn't see anything that bothered him. Cracker seemed calm too.

But as they walked on, he saw a young peasant girl at the edge of a rice paddy stand up quickly and scratch the back of her neck. Rick contemplated that. Could that be a signal to somebody? Camel had told him to listen to his intuition. Yet what were you going to do, arrest a girl for scratching her neck? Shoot her? The girl went back to work. Thirty or forty men, women, and children worked in the paddies, wearing conical straw hats and black pajamas. Cracker strained toward a chicken until Rick corrected her. He was glad now that he'd put her on a leash.

He called out, "Can someone make them get those chickens outta here? She's got a thing about chickens."

One of the guys started yelling at the villagers in Vietnamese. There was a lot of chatter among the villagers as they gathered the chickens and scooted them off.

Cracker suddenly knew it was all wrong. She stood very still and tried to figure out what was going on. She whined and growled softly. She looked up at Rick and yelped, but he didn't respond. She could feel it, a wave of tension rolling in from the peasants in the rice paddies. She squirmed on the leash, but Rick just tugged with annoyance and said, "No. No chickens!" The wave of tension was so strong, it was almost as powerful as the wind blasting from chopper blades when you climbed aboard. She pawed Rick, but again he just tugged with annoyance and said, "No!"

Rick frowned at Cracker. She was mostly a perfect dog, but these damn chickens drove her crazy. Then she sat in front of him and just stared at him. He remembered how she'd done that with the gourmet chicken at Fort Benning. He looked around, but everything was peaceful. It was almost like an illusion. And part of the illusion was that he could almost literally hear Camel's voice: *Listen to your intuition.*

Nineteen

HE SIGNALED THE LIEUTENANT. "SIR, THAT GIRL JUST stood up and scratched the back of her neck. Maybe that was a signal of some kind?"

The girl looked like she was about seven, if that. The lieutenant laughed. "You're getting paranoid, Dog Handler. Vietnam'll do that to you."

Rick pulled at Cracker. She refused to budge. This wasn't intuition anymore. It was common sense: Something was wrong. "Sir!" Rick called out again.

The lieutenant turned around, this time with impatience in his face. "Clear the village. I don't have time to be scared of a little girl. Let's just get this mission over with and get out of here."

The men gathered together all of the villagers and animals so Cracker could search the hootches.

Rick had no choice unless he wanted to disobey a direct order. He pulled on the leash with all his might and said, "Cracker, come!"

Cracker reluctantly stood up. Everything was all wrong. Even Rick was all wrong. Why wasn't he listening to her? She pawed Rick over and over, but he just kept hauling on her leash. What was wrong with him?

She turned her head quickly as she saw movement in the paddy. It was a rat! A big one! But then Rick was pulling on her again.

She gave the rat one last mournful glance. Rick looked over and saw the rat scurry away. Relief spread through him. Maybe that's why she was acting so nuts. They never should have let the dogs go after rats.

Cracker smelled gunpowder, felt tension, and heard faint sounds coming from some of the houses. She growled, lay down, and refused to get up.

The men all started laughing, and just like that, Rick felt a rush, exactly like the time in training right before he blew the booby trap. The laughing started to sound as if it were moving farther away from him, and everything suddenly seemed to go into slow motion. The second before it started, he thought, *Ambush.*

Villagers dropped to the ground all at once, as if

on signal, and a barrage of fire rang out. Machine guns! As Rick hit the dirt, he saw his slack man buckle over, blood spurting from his neck. Gunfire seemed to be coming from every direction. Rick let go of Cracker's leash and struggled to get his M-16 free. He couldn't see a single enemy, but gunfire burst from the houses. Charlie must have hidden in some tunnels under the huts. He blasted away at a hootch that had gunfire coming from it. A sudden sharp pain burned his right shin, but he didn't have time to check it. Cracker tried to crawl on top of him, no doubt to protect him. But it hampered his shooting ability, so he shoved her off and kept shooting.

He backed up in a crawl, shooting the whole time and not having the slightest idea if he was hitting anything. He set his rifle on auto even though he knew that meant he would use up his ammo more quickly. A bullet hit the ground right before him, kicking up mud in his eyes. It felt like acid. He tried wiping it out with his shirt, but his clothes were so filthy, he was just making it worse. He could barely see. He *couldn't* see.

Machine-gun fire exploded all around him. "Charlie doesn't have enough machine-gun ammo to keep this up long!" someone cried out. So Rick

Rick thought of Camel: *You have to try not to ask yourself whether you can do something. . . . You have to tell yourself, "I will do this."* He shouted out like a maniac, "I *will* push myself up!" And he did. He got up and shouted, "I gotta find my dog! Cracker!" The noises in the background seemed to fade. "Cracker!" He tried to call out, but his voice was weak and he fell to the ground. He could tell he might pass out soon. He said weakly, "I *will* do it," but then he couldn't. He lay back. "Doc. Doc. You gotta promise me you'll find my dog."

"We'll find your dog."

"You gotta promise. . . ." He had this weird feeling that nobody else was real, that maybe he was already dead and they were alive, and he was just watching. "Gotta get my dog," he said, or thought he said, but the approaching helicopter noise drowned his voice out. His head swam so badly, he didn't know if the doctor answered or not.

He wasn't even sure if that was his own voice saying, "Find Cracker. . . ."

wasn't surprised when the machine-gun aspect of the battle quickly ended.

Silence. Then a rocket-propelled grenade hit one of the APCs, blowing a hole in it. Pieces of the grenade ricocheted inside the APC. Someone screamed. The lieutenant must have called in for mortar fire, because a mortar exploded at the far end of the village. But Rick still had no idea what had happened. He couldn't see a thing. Who was dead? Who was alive? And then he felt sudden panic: Where was Cracker? He cried out, "Cracker!" When she didn't answer, he called out again, louder.

Guys were starting to talk in a wary way, but not panicked. His own panicked voice sounded out of place. He could tell everyone felt relatively safe now. Finally, his eyes cleared enough that he could see. They still stung like mad, but at least he could look around and make out a blur of movement and color.

But Rick couldn't see Cracker anywhere. He searched out the cleanest spot he could find on his shirt and rubbed at his eyes. That helped a little. But he still couldn't see Cracker. He knew she wouldn't have strayed far from him, but he wished he knew where she was. He looked toward the rice paddy but didn't see her. He doubted she would have gone toward the village, but he turned in that direction anyway, scanning the landscape. Some of the hootches were shot up so bad, they weren't really hootches anymore. They were just piles of thatch now.

The radioman was already calling for dust-offs. "Blood type O negative. That's Oscar November. Appears to be sunken chest wound. . . ."

Rick tried to stay calm as he slowly scoured the countryside for Cracker. He tried to push the panic down. Someone started to urge him onto his back, saying, "Let me have a look at that leg." The urging grew stronger, and another man helped, forcing him onto his back.

"What? What leg?" Rick said. "I gotta find my dog."

"Lie still, Private." It was the medic. Rick had that feeling again: *What the HELL is going on?* The medic applied a tourniquet and started an I.V.

He heard the radio operator saying, ". . . Hanski, Richard. Blood type A positive . . ."

Rick glanced at his leg and did a double take at the mess of blood and shrapnel. And just like that, it seemed as if the adrenaline of the battle drained from him and he could feel pain again. Intense pain. It was as if his eyes told him what his body didn't: He was injured. He saw one especially long piece of

metal sticking out of his leg, and he pulled it o shouting at the sharp pang.

The medic called to the radio operator, "Shrapn injury to popliteal artery."

". . . shrapnel injury to popliteal artery . . . ," th radioman echoed.

The medic called out, "Resected tendon!"

". . . resected tendon . . ."

The lieutenant leaned over Rick. "Don't worry son, we'll have you dusted off right away."

Rick said, "Sir, I can't find my dog. I can't leave without her." He grimaced. "Ah, man, my leg."

"We'll take care of your pain," said the medic.

Rick felt his head start to swim. Must have been morphine. He tried to push himself up. "No," he said. "No." He saw one of the guys shaking a villager, who chattered nearly hysterically in reply. Everybody was talking to somebody. English. Vietnamese. His eyelids felt heavy. "I gotta find my dog."

"Lie down, soldier. We'll find your dog."

Rick made a sudden great effort and pushed himself into a squat. "Ah!" he screamed. "Ah!" The pain from his leg shot through his entire body. He fell back down. "Oh, man. Oh, man."

The radio operator called out, "Dust-off's on the way!"

Twenty

WHEN THE FIRING STARTED, CRACKER TRIED TO STICK close to Rick, but after he pushed her away, a burst of gunfire divided them and she had no choice but to go left while he went right. The gunfire seemed to be chasing her, so she kept going left while the gunfire followed. Finally, she reached the rice paddy, where she crawled along a dike to get away. Then she'd spotted that rat again. He was worth about ten wieners in her opinion. And he was slow! She crushed him in her teeth, but just as she did, she felt a sharp jerk on her leash. A man had grabbed it. She tried to lunge, but he pulled so hard that she yelped and fell to the ground. Then something pounded on her head. The last thing she remembered was the rat slipping out of her mouth. . . .

She woke up in some kind of dark room that smelled of human urine. Several men were talking in excited voices. A touch of light trickled in from somewhere. Her neck hurt, and her head pounded. Several men stood looking at her, laughing and pointing, and she knew the men were talking about her. She recognized the man who had grabbed her leash earlier. He held a stick now and was acting as if he were hitting something. Then he rolled his eyes as if he were passing out. All the men laughed.

Then one man started yelling at her. The man with the stick raised it in the air, and another man began calling "dog" to her. She stood up unsteadily. The men laughed at her again. As the man with the stick relaxed, she bounded away, sailing past them all in one leap. The second she landed, she flew into the air again, speeding as fast as she could down a long tunnel that smelled of dirt and of people. She kept running, through tunnel after tunnel. Sometimes people would look up at her surprised. One room was filled with children who shouted excitedly as she ran through. She didn't know where she was going, just that she needed to keep moving.

She moved much more quickly than the men chasing her. She smelled fresh air and moved toward that, up and up through a slender tunnel until she spotted the sky.

She scurried out of the tunnel and tried to get her bearings, but she kept running. The sound of voices grew farther away. She didn't stop until she reached a jungle, and then she stood perfectly still for a moment, hearing and smelling nothing but jungle noises and jungle smells. A bird called from a tree. She bristled a little but knew she had more important things to do.

Cracker always knew what direction was what, but she felt something unfamiliar now: uncertainty. She *always* knew. But now she didn't know, not for sure. If only her head would stop hurting. Why was it hurting? She tried to shake the pounding out of her head, but it wouldn't go away. She turned to the left, then the right, then behind herself. She used to know in what direction Willie lived. But now she didn't. She turned around again, then decided to go that way. She felt better after traveling a distance. This must be the right way. Right? She was thirsty and hungry, and the leash dangling from her neck annoyed her, but she felt confident again.

She did feel anxious about being separated from Rick, but she felt confident about where she'd last seen him. She hoped he was still there. There was a moment that day when she thought she'd passed the same place twice, and she lost confidence and whined. But she kept going. She needed to find Rick. She trotted at the edge of a rice paddy. All the peasants in their big hats looked up and called to one another, pointing her out. She didn't understand a word they were saying, but she knew she couldn't let them catch her. A couple of them shouted something and started running in her direction. It was easy to outdistance them, even with the dogs she heard baying behind her. They were so far away, and she was so fast and strong. Her legs were unaffected by uncertainty.

She understood now that she needed to avoid humans. Nobody could be trusted except Rick and people Rick trusted. She began moving more slowly but still steadily, making sure nobody saw her. The jungles took longer to move through, but unlike the paddies and villages, they were empty—of humans at least. Once, she did hear a human voice, but it was far away. Another time she stopped when she smelled one of the smells that Rick had trained her to respond to. She sat down automatically and pondered what to do. She could hear the wind passing over a string. She stood up and moved slowly until the noise grew louder and the smell of gunpowder filled her nose. Then she simply walked around the string and the gunpowder.

She just wished she knew the direction for sure the way she used to. She pushed down any doubt and searched her mind for certainty. For a moment she just about had it. But the pounding in her head wouldn't stop and she lost the certainty. When she was thirsty, she looked around until she found a trickle of water seeping up beneath some rocks. Rick never let her drink unless he gave her the water. But she was thirsty, so she drank, looking around guiltily every so often. The water tasted clean and fresh, so she drank as much as she could before she started to feel the pull of Rick. She had to get to him. He needed her. She helped him. She was important. She trotted on and on, even when her stomach growled with hunger. Hunger was important, but not like thirst. She couldn't go on without water. But food, she could last awhile without that.

The time came when the sky was dark and her body began to ache, and she didn't think she could go farther. She'd walked long distances before but had never run so much in her life. She sniffed around the dark jungle. She knew she could see better at night than Rick or Willie, because they always moved around comically in the dark, with their hands in front of them to feel their way. That seemed funny to her sometimes. But this darkness was so dark that her eyes couldn't gather enough light to know what was around her. Cracker could hear, though, and she could smell, and so she had a pretty good idea of where she was and all that was around her. She knew the size of the leaves hanging from the trees, how disintegrated the leaves on the ground were, how softly the wind blew—everything except what color it all was. She felt ants crawling on her back. She walked a little farther, to an area that didn't seem to have so many ants, though she knew they would come for her.

She sniffed around, first raising her head the way she'd been taught, but she didn't smell anything unusual in the wind. Then she lowered her nose and sniffed the ground, the way she'd been taught not to do. She pawed at the dirt, clearing away a nice area of dirt to lie in. Even when she lay down, the anxiety of finding Rick still ran strong through her, but the feeling of needing sleep was even stronger. Before she closed her eyes, she raised her nose once more but smelled nothing special. She let herself sleep.

Twenty-one

Rick's vision blurred as some guys loaded him onto the dust-off. He thought he was only drowsy, but he must have passed out, because all of a sudden he saw that the chopper had landed. Even in his drowsy state, he could see how well organized everything was. Emergency personnel had already been alerted to what kind of injured were on board. Rick watched his slack man, who looked dead, being rushed off. A couple of guys carried Rick to an operating room, and then he was gone.

He woke up in a Quonset hut with a door on each side. One of the doors appeared to lead outside, the other to a hallway. A couple of guys were flirting with a nurse. A young Asian doctor stood over him. For a second he thought he might have been captured.

Then the doctor said, "Hi, I'm Dr. Kanamori. How are you feeling?"

"I lost my dog. She didn't dust off with me."

"Excuse me?"

"I'm a dog handler."

"I'm sure someone took care of her. Let's talk about your injury, and then we'll get to your dog. In laymen's terms, shrapnel pierced your right artery and tendon. We needed to take a piece of your left artery and sew it into your right one. We'll keep you here a couple of weeks, but after that, it looks like you're going stateside for rehab."

"You mean I'm going home?"

"You sure are. Congratulations."

"But my dog. I'm a handler with the 67th IPSD. My dog was lost when they dusted me off."

The doctor paused, then turned to a nurse and gestured her over. "Linda, this is a dog handler from the 67th IPSD. His dog didn't dust off with him. Can you check to see if the animal was found?"

"Yes, doctor." She hurried off.

The doctor smiled at Rick. "Don't worry, we'll find your dog." He sounded sympathetic, but Rick could tell he was in a hurry. "Now get some rest," the doctor said before continuing down the aisle.

Rick called out, "Do you know what happened

to my slack man? His name was Rafael."

The doctor turned reluctantly. Rick wanted to say "Never mind," but the doctor had already started talking. "Rafael didn't make it. I'm sorry." Rick waited for more, maybe the cause of death, but all the doctor said was, "He didn't suffer." Then he began talking to the next wounded soldier.

Rick felt weird in his head, trying to get it all straight. For one thing, how come he felt worse about Cracker than about Rafael? He lay still and waited as his head cleared. Some guys were playing cards. He finally was able to push himself up. A guy glanced at him.

"Poker?"

"No, thanks."

Rick lay back, waiting for someone to tell him about Cracker. But hours passed and nobody came.

By the end of the day Rick's head felt fairly clear. But the clearer his head became, the more he could feel exactly where it was, "it" being the worry about Cracker. It was not in his heart, because that would be his left side. It was in his chest. Maybe it tended toward his left: nah, just his imagination. It all seemed unreal—the hospital, the guys playing poker and laughing. It felt irrelevant or something. What the hell was he doing here? What was everybody thinking? He looked around at the guys playing cards, reading magazines. What did they think? That everything was okay now? That they were gonna go on and have great lives or something?

One of the cardplayers met his eyes. "Hey, bud, wanna play?"

Rick shook his head. "Uh-uh. But thanks." The guy shrugged, and a couple of them raised their eyebrows at each other, like they thought Rick was *dinky dau*.

Rick looked at the guy who'd invited him to play. He felt like he knew the guy inside out, though he'd never met him. Mr. Socializer. That would have been Dan Devine at his high school. Last he'd heard, Devine had been drafted.

Rick still felt the thing in his chest, the ache, the guilt. He wondered whether he should have tied Cracker to his leg. But everything had happened so fast. He went over the ambush in his head, over and over until night fell, and the next day he did the same thing all over again. The other guys in the hospital ignored him.

Someone had sent his bag of stuff to the hospital. He went through it and came upon his bundle of letters. He counted Willie's: thirty-seven. Jeez, the kid was dedicated. Then the idea hit him. Maybe

Willie could help. Anyone who could write thirty-seven letters couldn't hurt. If they each wrote thirty-seven, that would make seventy-four.

One of the nurses came to help walk him up and down the ward to prevent blood clots and help stretch his tendon. They told him that the first few days he'd be on crutches, then on a cane. But he had to keep moving.

He asked the nurse, "Can I get some stationery? Lots of it."

"Sure thing. Especially if you promise to keep exercising that leg for the next few weeks. Heel to floor! It'll keep your tendon stretched out."

"Deal. I gotta write some letters and find my dog."

"Oh, I heard about you." She even stopped to stroke his face. "You poor thing. Don't worry, hon, I'll get you all the stationery you want."

She walked him back to his bed. The guy next to him said, "What, is that some kind of trick for picking up girls?"

Rick didn't reply.

All that week he wrote to anyone he could think of. Occasionally, he stopped to walk up and down the ward, even on his own with the cane. He knew the faster he recovered, the faster he'd be let out of this place. The nurse who'd first walked him had explained the situation to the other nurses. They got him addresses, contacts. He wrote Willie, explained the situation. He wrote Camel. He wrote his parents. His sister. His sister's dissertation chair. Twenty-Twenty. His congressman. The nurses' congressmen. Everyone he could think of. How was that for applying himself? How was that for being a specialist? A dog-finding specialist.

It took him a long time to write each letter, because his handwriting stank and because he'd never done something like this before. In fact, it was kind of embarrassing, because one of the nurses had to show him how to format a letter properly. But it felt good as she leaned over him.

The nurses got so involved, they even had some clerical personnel typing up letters. The other guys in the ward got jealous—how could some guy who was *dinky dau* over a dog be getting all the ladies' attention? Rick basked in it a little, but mostly he got excited. According to one nurse, he'd mobilized the whole staff about it. If that wasn't a specialist, there wasn't any such thing. If that wasn't applying himself, what was? And the nurses practically competed to be the one to exercise him every day, cooing to him about his dog. He felt a little like his grandfather with the cane, but the girls cooing in his ear sure was nice.

Twenty-two

WHEN CRACKER OPENED HER EYES, SHE COULD TELL it was later than she usually woke up. The pounding in her head was softer now. A few intense beams of sunlight stretched downward through the trees. Everything looked just as she'd figured it had the night before. It looked like many of the jungles she'd seen since she'd come to this place with Rick. Anxiety gripped her hard at the thought of Rick. She got up, stretched, shook off, stretched again, and began to run. She raced through the jungle, even though Rick had taught her never to rush. She had to find him.

Eventually, she needed to stop because she could no longer ignore her thirst. She pushed at rocks and dug at roots, but she didn't find any water. She smelled the air and also listened to it. She saw a snake and knew to back away. Then she listened again and heard a soft drip of water through the bush to her right. She went that way and found a few drops falling from some rocks. It wasn't much, but it wet her mouth enough to help her move on.

She felt a little sick but couldn't stop now. Maybe she was hungry, or maybe it was because she drank from one of those rice paddies the day before. She thought again about how Rick always scolded her when she tried to drink from anywhere but his helmet. But his helmet wasn't here, and she was thirsty.

But there was another reason she felt sick, and the sick feeling kept growing stronger. She could tell, she just knew, that Rick was no longer where she had last seen him. At the same time she didn't know where this was. Again she pushed away a feeling that she was passing the same place twice, that maybe she was lost. She paused and whined again, but there was nobody to hear her. She needed to keep going. But which way?

After a while she struck out in the way she felt she must have seen him last. The sun was already setting when she finally arrived.

She slowed down as she neared the place. *Easy.* This was the place that had caused all this trouble in the first place. She peeked out of the jungle and saw people just leaving the field. She crouched down so they wouldn't see her—humans here seemed to get quite excited when they did. She could smell freshly dug dirt, and she could smell decaying bodies underneath that dirt. But no matter how much she concentrated, she couldn't smell Rick.

There were other smells, however, that interested her. The smell of chickens, for instance. She lay down and waited for darkness. But when darkness fell, a bunch of men dressed in black went through the homes talking to people. Sometimes she heard shouting or a gunshot. When the men left, the village was silent of human sounds. Yet she sensed that people were awake. She waited more.

After the men had been gone a long while, she crept along the edge of the field and stopped at a small house. There were chickens underneath, and they were sleeping. She lunged and grabbed one, setting off a ruckus of chickens and pigs and humans and who knew what else. She just ran and ran, back into the jungle with the chicken in her mouth. She knew nobody would catch her. She heard human voices crying after her.

She ripped into the chicken's throat and ate the insides and even some of the feathers. The feeling of ripping into this chicken flooded her with energy. She loved the taste of blood. For a moment she forgot everything else in the world except the feeling of life flooding through her. She crunched on the bones, and when she was finished, she felt a little disappointed to have no more food. She always felt that way when she finished eating. But she was stronger than before.

She went deeper into the forest and fell asleep. In the morning she felt better. The pounding had almost gone away. She felt confidence returning. She knew what to do: head back to where she lived with Rick. The trucks they'd come in had made a clear path through the jungle. People were already using the path, but whenever she saw or heard a person, she simply stepped off the path and waited until they went by. Then she moved again. Later, when there was no jungle to hide her, she had only a small window of time to travel if she wanted to avoid humans. She didn't want to wait, but she knew she had to. At night there seemed to be more human activity than during the days. During the day the humans worked in the fields, but at night she saw a different type of person, the ones with guns kind of like Rick's. They were everywhere at night. Some wore uniforms and some didn't.

Every so often she passed a hole in the ground that reminded her of the hole she'd been in when she was captured, and she would run fast from the hole. Once, she passed another village and waited until everybody was asleep before stealing a chicken again and running off to eat it. Then she ran until early morning, when people began waking up.

She felt a little more hopeful now, because she knew that she was getting closer.

Then she finally saw the place where she had lived with Rick. Happiness swelled up in her, and she broke into an unthinking gallop. She didn't stop until she was right at the place.

It was empty.

Twenty-three

THAT IS, IT WASN'T EMPTY. THERE WERE PEOPLE who weren't Rick's friends going through the garbage, gathering pieces of wood or metal into baskets, and generally swarming over the camp, taking everything they could. She saw men yanking at wooden stakes stuck into the ground. She saw children dragging huge cans. She recognized some of the people from before, when she and Rick used to watch the locals pick through the trash.

But Rick and his friends were gone. Someone spotted her and started talking in an excited voice, but nobody moved. Instead of running off, which was her first instinct, she charged toward where Rick's home had been. People scattered as she snarled at anyone who didn't move out of her way.

When she reached Rick's former home, she stood still a second to smell. She found where his bed had been. She could smell him. She whined . . . but turned around just as several men were trying to creep toward her with big wooden sticks in their hands. She decided it was time to go.

She ran off past the rice paddy and didn't stop until she'd reached a jungle. Then she lay down behind a canopy of leaves and didn't move. She just thought. She knew she was in the right place, because she'd smelled Rick's bed and because she just knew. Except for when her head pounded, she always knew exactly where she was in relation to where she'd been. She didn't know how she knew. She could still hear, in the distance, the sounds of people ripping up the camp. Something exploded. Someone screamed. Nothing unusual.

Cracker's mouth had grown parched, but she ignored it. Her stomach grumbled, but it didn't matter. She lowered her head to the ground and thought about all the different places she'd been with Rick and whether he might have gone to one of those places. The only other place they'd stayed a long time was "Tonsonoo," when they'd first arrived. They'd been there another time for a visit to a man who poked her for some reason. Rick called him "vet." She saw vets all the time since being in this place. But then there was also "Benwa" and the man who scratched her ears so well. Should she go there?

She hardly moved until night, and then she crawled all the way to the camp, just the way Rick had taught her to move when there was danger. The camp was now truly empty. She lay where Rick's bed had been, which was now an open field with a few bits of paper flying in the wind like moths. She didn't feel like moving, even when she saw bugs the size of mice scurrying across the field.

She ached for Rick. He was the source of everything. When morning came and she heard people approaching, she ran back into the forest. Again, as thirsty and hungry as she was, she didn't search for food and water. And again when night fell, she returned to the camp and longed for Rick, but her longing was different from the previous day's. Hope was draining from her. She remembered that Willie had never come for her, and now she wondered whether Rick would ever come for her. She didn't understand why people left her. What had she done? Her tongue was getting so dry, it was starting to stick to her mouth.

The next morning when daytime came and just a few people arrived to search through the rubble, she ran again to hide in the jungle. But when night came, she felt too weak to walk to the camp. Her tongue was changing. It was bigger and harder—it didn't curl right anymore. But she didn't feel like searching for water. She felt like just lying there, the way those dogs in the pound had just lain there. At the time she had wondered why they had lain there that way, but now she understood. She didn't care if she died. She didn't want to be killed by any of those people, though; instead, she would just lie here and die of thirst. She laid her head on her front paws, and her body shook a bit as it did when she whimpered. But no whimpers came from her.

When morning arrived, she was still alive, but her tongue had changed even more. It hung out of her mouth, bloated and unbendable and dry, like a dead thing that was attached to her. She didn't move, for there was nowhere to go and nothing to do. There was danger everywhere, but even if she could avoid all dangers, what would be the point? Willie had let her go, and Rick had abandoned her. She could feel that she was closer to death today than yesterday. Her tongue was useless, and her throat felt like that time she swallowed a rock and Willie's father had to take her someplace to get it out. And she was having trouble getting air into her: Every time she inhaled, she felt as if she couldn't take in quite enough air. The trees seemed to wobble, but not really the way they wobbled when the wind hit them. She saw sparkles in the air. As she lay, dying, she saw a man with a box click it at her. She didn't know what that meant, and she didn't care.

Then rain began to drizzle from the sky. She could see it filling a hole in the dirt near her. Despite everything, the rain in the hole beckoned her. She watched the drops splash occasionally into the hole. Occasionally, a drop fell on her tongue. She pushed herself to her feet and almost fell over. She waited a moment, but she couldn't resist the chance to live longer. For what, she didn't know. But she went to the hole and dropped her tongue inside. She felt her tongue soften as it sopped up water. She waited for the hole to fill again as she hung her tongue in it. A soft foam filled her mouth. Her tongue began to soften. But the drizzle ceased, and her mouth began to dry out again.

Later that day she heard a noise and saw a boy standing near the edge of the jungle. Her vision still wobbled. For a moment she wasn't even sure she saw him. He was staring at her and saying something, but not in the excited tone that those other people had used with her. He was holding a bucket.

She growled softly but didn't move as he set the bucket halfway between them and then stepped back. Then she vaguely remembered seeing him around camp. He was one of the people who went through the garbage, not one of Rick's friends. But she remembered that Rick had thrown him some cans of food once. He was dark, small, and slender. He had only one leg, and he walked with a stick. She wondered if he had come to kill her.

"Name Quan," he said. "Name Quan." He patted his chest. "Quan." He pointed to the bucket. She knew what "name" was, sort of. "You hunt? You help Quan?"

She didn't know what he was babbling about. But she could smell food in the bucket. Cracker knew danger, and she knew opportunity, and she knew that sometimes they could exist in the same place. Despite everything, that food in the bucket beckoned her. She walked over; the food tasted new, different, but she dipped her entire nose and mouth in, causing a sensation almost like pain and pleasure at the same time. Then she swallowed over and over until the bucket was empty. She could almost feel the food spreading throughout her whole body.

When she was finished, the boy was waiting patiently. He said again, "You help Quan?"

She shook herself out. Her whole body felt stiff, the way it had after that first long ride to this strange land. She started to peek out of the jungle, but the boy said something excitedly. She looked at him curiously. He put a cigarette butt in his mouth and lit it with a lighter, just like Rick used to.

Cracker waited. She didn't expect anything at all, she just waited. She felt her body strengthening. She didn't trust the boy, but on the other hand, he had just helped her. So she waited. Then she heard someone behind him shouting, and she knew it was about her.

She ran off, alone again.

Twenty-four

CRACKER HAD TO FIND RICK. SHE LISTENED TO
every sound she could hear, smelled every smell she
could smell, and—most importantly—searched inside
of herself for where Rick could be. But she couldn't
find an answer. Mostly, all she heard and smelled
were birds and monkeys, which she admitted were
pretty interesting. But they weren't Rick. She could
head for that Tonsonoo place, but she had no idea
if he was there. And many people lived there, and
people were dangerous. Anyway, she didn't think he
was there. She could just tell.

She thought about the Camel man. He and his
friends had petted her and called her "good girl."
And she could never forget the man who was so
good at scratching her ears. She and Rick had been

several places with him, but they had started out at "Benwa." Everybody at Benwa was nice to her. She stood up and faced in the direction of Benwa. She turned her ears this way and that and raised her nose into the wind. She stood very still and concentrated on Benwa. Then she decided. Once she decided, that was that. Benwa it was. She walked all day in what she thought was the right direction. Her head hurt less, yet occasionally, the pounding came back, and she doubted she was going in the right direction. But she ignored the doubt, stopping only for water. At night she rested in the jungle. She pushed deep into a bush, letting some twigs jab her. She lay down and stayed still. She thought of Rick saying, *Easy, Cracker, easy.*

In the morning she ran off. She kept running and running, forgetting the word "easy." She knew she was making too much noise, and at some point she heard human voices crying out. She ran as fast as she could. Running, running, running. Soon the forest fell silent again. She hid in some bushes but didn't lie down. She just stood there. *Easy.*

Finally, she lay down and slept, and in the morning she continued to Benwa.

Twenty-five

THE FIRST WEEK HAD PASSED QUICKLY, AND RICK actually started to feel optimistic. By the time the second week passed, he figured that when he went stateside, he would mobilize the whole rehab clinic. Or if they weren't as helpful as the staff here, he would do it all himself. On the other hand, mixed with his optimism was doubt. Could a dog—even a great dog like Cracker—survive this long out there in the jungle?

A few days before Rick was to be shipped back for stateside rehab, his mouth dropped open as U-Haul–U-Haul!—walked up to the bed carrying a manila file. He patted Rick's good leg just like a friend might. Was the universe going completely insane? U-Haul hadn't bothered to stop by even once since Rick had been injured.

"I've got news," the sergeant said. Rick hesitated—in Nam "news" usually meant "bad news."

"You found Cracker," Rick said. The only question was: Dead or alive?

"All we know is she's been spotted. Somebody found this near our base." He handed Rick the file.

Rick opened it to find a black-and-white picture of a bedraggled Cracker lying in a forest, her tongue hanging out of her mouth but a dull spark of life still in her eyes. He cried out, "Cracker!"

"There are some Vietnamese photographers who travel alone, taking pictures of the war for Charlie to use as propaganda. They hang the photos on trees sometimes. I tell ya, it's pretty damn bizarre to be walking through a forest and see a bunch of pictures hanging from the trees. A guy from the 199th Light Infantry found this."

Cracker looked strange—limp but definitely alive. "I gotta get out of here and save her!" cried Rick. It was possible she was alive. He searched the picture for more information but didn't find anything. Then he searched his intuition and found nothing. Or rather, he found something: He thought she was dead.

Rick pushed himself all the way up. "Sergeant, they want to send me home. Is there any way I can stay to search for Cracker–?" He'd started to say *Cracker's body* but stopped himself.

U-Haul shook his head. He seemed defeated. "I'm afraid not. The 67th has stood down."

"Stood down?" That meant they'd been deactivated!

"Our side of the war is winding down, you know that."

"But, Sergeant—"

"Did you know the Vietnamese call this the 'American War'?"

"Sarge, I gotta find her."

"Rick . . ." Rick fell silent; U-Haul had never called him "Rick" before. He braced himself for more bad news as U-Haul stared at Cracker's picture. "You gotta move on."

Rick knew the sarge was probably right, but he said, "No. No, there's no other dog like her. If any dog could make it, it would be her." And as he said it, he started to believe again.

The sergeant's jowls seemed to be sagging. Then he seemed furious. "Lanski, just thank your lucky stars you're in one piece. Twenty-Twenty lost his arm."

"Aw, jeez. Jeez. I'm sorry." And he *was* really sorry. Yet he still couldn't stop. He said, "But, Sarge, about Cracker. I know her. She knows me. If she's alive, we could find each other out there."

U-Haul shook his head. "You're goin' mental, Lanski. Good luck in the world." And he walked off.

Rick lay back again and held up the picture of Cracker. It was her, all right. But she looked like a mess. He wondered how long Cracker could survive out there, especially now that the platoon had stood down. She wouldn't know where to go.

Twenty-six

Rick was rehabbing stateside, at Fitzsimons Army Hospital just outside of Denver. He rode an army medevac plane back. Racks of bunks filled the back of the plane for the more badly hurt soldiers. Rick mostly sat up in one of the seats or took walks up and down the plane. He knew the more he walked, the faster he would heal. He hated feeling like an invalid. He didn't know what more he could do to find Cracker when he healed, though.

Except for him, everyone had seemed glad to be leaving. It should have been a happy day for him, but all he could think of was Cracker and how he was getting farther away from her. He had looked at her picture once more, but then he couldn't look at it again. During takeoff he had stared out the window at the tarmac, remembering back to one day when nothing much was going on. Cody had suggested they get their fortunes told by one of the locals who begged around camp. It was just for fun. The woman always said she was a fortune teller before her village got bombed out. Cody paid her five bucks, and she had moaned and held her head— you could see it was a big con job. But Cody took it all seriously. She spoke pretty good English and told him he was going to be a senator someday. Rick had laughed at that. She got mad at his laughing and told him she saw a net. She moaned again and closed her eyes. "A net!" At first Rick had thought she was saying the name "Annette." Then she looked at him haughtily and said, "And you are caught in the net!" And now, even as the plane flew through the air, he finally believed the fortune teller.

From the sky, he saw Vietnam spread out, more pockmarked than when he'd flown in. He'd heard that at least some of those pockmarks were not bomb craters, but actually craters from burnt-out latrines. He pressed his head to the window. He had the crazy idea that he might spot Cracker down there. But he couldn't even spot the village where he'd last seen her. He'd begged everybody within hearing distance to let him stay to search for

278

Cracker. But, basically, the army seemed to b
with him and with her.

His first night in the hospital after his leg
tion, he'd dreamed he was rising farther and f
above Vietnam, looking down at the jungle
calling, "Cracker! Cracker!" He'd risen highe
higher, until he could see the whole earth, spai
in the cities and dark in the jungles. He'd callec
called and at one point had been rewarded w
desperate bark. Then he woke up.

He realized he'd been trying to keep sometl
buried in him, and that something was anger.
righteous indignation. Anger. The army didn't
about the dogs. He doubted the army cared ab
even him, Rick. They were done with Cracker, a
they were done with Rick. They couldn't work ai
more. And that was all the army cared about.

He rubbed his eyes and forehead. Cracker was
smart dog. She might make it. He'd left word wi
the other handlers to watch for her. He thougl
maybe whoever had taken the picture might have fe
and watered her. But even if she made it to America
hands, he didn't know what would become of her.

He caught a last glimpse of Vietnam as the plane
reached the ocean. From the airplane window, the
faraway ocean waves made the water seem to quiver,

like a swarm of writhing insects. Everything looked like insects. The Vietnam effect. He caught a flash of Saigon, but then all he could see was water. It was over. For him, the war was over. Rick had as much trouble comprehending that concept as he'd had comprehending when the war had begun for him.

His parents flew down to visit him at Fitzsimons during his recovery a couple of times, but all he could talk to them about was his dog. They brought him food—it tasted okay—and told him about the hardware store, the neighborhood, and his friends, but none of it interested him. He saw the way they looked at each other, like maybe he was a little nuts. He was interested in just two things: finding Cracker and exercising rabidly so he would rehabilitate faster. For some reason, he figured that if he could get out of the army sooner, he could somehow save Cracker.

"You know you always have a job waiting," his father said. "When you're ready, of course."

"Dad, I gotta find my dog."

His parents just sighed.

He spent all his extra time writing to the same people: congressmen and senators, his mayor and governor, army officials and buddies, Twenty-Twenty and Twenty's uncle, and Willie, who'd already written him back twice, saying he would write as many

letters as he could. Besides Willie, everybody he wrote to was probably getting sick of him. He'd even written to the president of the United States. Hey, the president knew he'd crossed the border, right? Camel had said so. So maybe he'd remember him and his dog. One day he even wrote thirty-seven letters, the same number Willie had written him before he was injured. His hand was so sore after that that he could barely hold his fork at dinner that night. And yet nothing had come of any of it so far.

He was a star patient. He walked and stretched whether asked to or not, and by the end of a month he was processed out with no more fanfare than the day he'd checked out of the hospital a few years ago with appendicitis.

Twenty-seven

CRACKER RAISED HER NOSE TOWARD THE EMPTY SKY
and smelled nothing special, saw nothing special,
and felt nothing special. She whimpered and
moaned. Then she started trotting again toward
"Benwa." She'd found a lot of water to drink today,
but now her stomach was upset. And she was hungry.
And lonely.

She stopped again, forgetting all her sad
thoughts. Just a few leaps away lay a fat, gray lizard.
She took a step forward, and the lizard started scurrying off. Cracker sped after it.

She forgot all else for the moment. She wanted
to catch this lizard. Her muscles felt full of energy,
and her hurting heart found a reason to live, simply
in chasing this lizard. The lizard was fast, but she felt

like it was practically standing still. When it tried to climb a tree, she leapt through the air and managed to swipe her paw against its body. It began running again, and she chased it. When she was just about to jump on it for a kill, it stopped suddenly and turned around, hissing at her. She paused. She had no idea if it was dangerous or not. With humans, she always knew immediately if she could take them or not in a fight. But this was something new. She wasn't afraid, though. On the contrary, she felt almost deliriously happy. She snarled. The animal hissed. She pounced, planning to land by its side so she could hit it with her paw before grabbing its throat.

But it whipped around so quickly that it was facing her again, and they were back where they started. She tried again with the same results. Then she just ran straight at it, hitting it aside with her right paw and grabbing its throat when it fell over. Her mouth filled with blood. She whipped her head back and forth over and over in a frenzy.

The blood-smell was incredibly strong. She ripped at the stomach and swallowed the strong-smelling guts. She'd never tasted anything so good. She ate until she was full, and then she lay down. The jungle was warm, and it felt good to sleep.

When she woke again, it was already getting

dark. She was full of optimism as she set off, occasionally stepping around one of the things that Rick had taught her to avoid. She would find him.

Sometimes she moved of her own volition; other times she was pulled by a force. Her stomach rumbled constantly. But when she reached Benwa and saw all the activity, she broke into a gallop. She stopped just outside of camp and watched the men at the base. These men were like Rick. But they weren't Rick.

An American soldier yelled out, "Hey, that looks like a scout dog!"

Another soldier said, "Check her ear."

The soldier walked cautiously toward her. She growled, but softly, and stepped back. Rick had taught her to tolerate guys like him. Even though Rick was gone, all that training they'd done together made her know that it was important to tolerate certain types of people. So she stood very still as the man checked her ear and said, "Yup, she's one of ours. Seventy-two AO."

Cracker studied the soldiers. They were dressed just like Rick.

Cracker didn't know for certain whether these new events were good or bad. She just recognized the uniform of the man who now picked up her leash as the same one guys like Rick wore. Uniforms were easy to recognize. This guy seemed like a friend. But she didn't long for him the way she longed for Rick. She didn't understand any of this. She just wanted Rick.

The man started talking like Rick. "Easy. Easy, girl." So she sat, though she growled very softly.

The one man said to another, "She must have got loose somehow. By the look of her coat, it's been a while." The man gazed into the jungle. "Of course, even a day in the wrong jungle can get you looking pretty bad." He petted her head. "I got a shepherd at home."

Cracker thought he was an average petter. But she could tell he was a good man. *Good man.*

The men walked off, Cracker heeling with the man holding her leash. She followed them because now they were all she had. They put her in a windowless room with a bowl of warm water. She paced and paced, urinated on the floor, paced more, and raked the door.

Finally, the good man returned with another. "Everything's pretty disorganized," he was saying. He petted her again. "We couldn't find her records, but she's got the tattoo, so she's definitely one of ours."

"What happens to her next?" said the other man.

The first man lowered his voice, as if Cracker wouldn't understand if he talked softly. She listened intently, though of course she couldn't understand. "They're sending a few of the dogs home if they pass the health exams, but they're either giving the rest to the South Vietnamese Army or putting them down."

"The army's putting down its own dogs?"

"Yeah. It's the Vietnamization, man. They're leaving behind or destroying unnecessary equipment."

"So what do we do with her?"

"There're a couple of scout dog platoons here right now. They just stood down. We'll give her to one of them."

Cracker looked eagerly back and forth between the two men. She knew they were talking about her. She stood up and wagged her tail. She licked the good man's hand. He and the other man didn't look at her, but rather into the wall, as if they saw something special there. She looked at it but saw just a wall.

"Helluva war," one said.

The next few days went okay. She got kenneled and fed, and somebody even brushed her. One of the original men who'd found her came and petted her sometimes. She kept waiting to see Rick again. But mostly all she saw was a bunch of bored guys throwing food into her kennel and occasionally cleaning it out.

Twenty-eight

EVERY DAY THERE WERE FEWER DOGS. CRACKER DIDN'T know where they were going. When there were hardly any dogs left, a man moved her into a different kennel. At the far end she saw Bruno! She barked at him and he barked back. She twirled around and he twirled back. Then Cody walked up. She barked hysterically. Cody stared at her for a second, and she heard him say, "Hold on, Bruno." Bruno whined.

Cody ran closer and looked into her eyes. "Unbelievable." He flung open her gate, and she nearly knocked him over with joy. He hugged her, and they rushed over to Bruno's kennel. She and Bruno broke into a run, then ran and ran, Cody calling after them. Then they both realized they should turn back, and they ran and ran back toward Cody, where Bruno jumped all over him as he laughed. All that morning they played and ran together on the obstacle course and through the whole base.

Then they walked over to where some of the familiar guys and their dogs were standing around. But everybody seemed sad. Bruno stuck his tail between his legs. Cracker and Bruno stood together, unsure what was going on. All of a sudden a bunch of the guys were crying. Cody knelt down and held Bruno to him, Cody's body heaving.

Cody leashed Bruno and handed him to another soldier, who put him in a crate. Some guys carried the crate to a truck where some other dogs in crates had already been loaded. What was going on? When the truck was full of dogs, it drove off, the guys crying and the dogs staring at them. Cody and Bruno met eyes. They stared at each other until the truck rolled out of sight.

After a few weeks at the kennel somebody leashed Cracker and took her to the veterinarian. She remembered this vet from their old home where she'd lived with Rick. He was Rick's friend. He prodded her sometimes, and once he gave her a treat.

She was poked and prodded more, and then somebody walked her down a hallway. She happened to glance into one room, where she saw a pile of dead dogs. The sight shocked her so much, she stopped walking and, without thinking, pulled on her leash to get away. Then somebody put her in a kennel outside, and even though she got food and water, nobody paid much attention to her. There were a few other dogs in the kennel, but not many.

Every so often one of the dogs left and didn't come back. One day an unfamiliar man finally came to get her. "Cracker! Heel!"

She dragged her legs as he pulled her into a building. She passed another room full of dead dogs. She wanted to bite this man. He pulled her down a hallway. Farther down the hallway the vet she recognized was leaning against a wall with his eyes closed. Cracker sniffed the air. The air was filled with death. "Hey, Doc," said the man pulling Cracker's leash. "You okay?"

"I didn't become a veterinarian for this," he said.

"How many did you euthanize today?"

"Twenty."

They both looked at Cracker. She didn't know what this exchange was about, whether it was good or bad. She wagged her tail to show them she meant no harm. She remembered those dogs jumping up and down in the pound. She wondered whether she should jump up and down. Instead, she sat. Whenever she sat for Rick, he petted her and said, "Good girl." Now both these men reached down, petted her head, and said, "Good girl."

Sitting down always made people happy!

The vet took her to another room and stuck yet another sharp thing into her. She wondered why some of these humans liked to stick sharp things in her. She wondered where Rick was. She wondered if he was coming for her. . . . She wondered if anyone would feed her soon. . . . She wondered . . .

Twenty-nine

RICK WAS FLYING INTO O'HARE, WHERE HIS PARENTS would be meeting him. It was a commercial flight, but there were several DEROSing vets on board. He'd decided to wear his uniform, like a couple of the others. When Rick's plane was just about to touch down in Chicago, the captain came on the plane's P.A. system. "Welcome home to our brave soldiers from Vietnam. We'd like to ensure your well-being and have been asked to remind you that to avoid incident over your status as Vietnam veterans, you are advised to remove your uniforms before you deplane or soon thereafter. In the meantime, the temperature in Chicago is a chilly 28 degrees, with winds at twenty miles per hour. We're expecting to touch down a few minutes early. It's been a pleasure being your pilot."

The soldiers all looked at one another. Rick didn't even have an extra set of clothes with him. He was so worried about Cracker that he hadn't even thought about politics. He saw one guy grab his bag from the overhead compartment and take it into the lavatory, emerging a few minutes later in civvies.

Rick hadn't even thought of civvies. Cracker was all that mattered. He thought, *This is what time does. It changes what matters.* He smiled ruefully at himself, Rick the Philosopher. Rick knew that some things would stick through time. This Cracker thing wouldn't go away, ever.

As the plane closed in on land, the sun hung in some strange spot, creating the illusion that the streets below were like mirrors or something. Must have had something to do with the sun reflecting off the tops of the cars, Rick figured. As the plane lowered, he saw its shadow to one side on the ground, first small and then getting larger. It seemed like the ghost of Cracker running alongside the plane but finally merging with the plane. By the time they landed, it looked like what it was: just a simple shadow.

Rick saw neatly cut grass edging the runway. Weird, after all that elephant grass in Nam.

The ache. It had gotten worse every mile he'd traveled farther away from Vietnam. When your heart belonged somewhere different from where your body was, it made everything depressing. Rick the Philosopher again.

As he deplaned in Chicago, he held his head high. Walking away from the plane he limped a bit—what he pictured as a tough guy's limp. He tried to close off his inner ear like a dog could, but sometimes something broke through. Like a couple walking together but clearly arguing, the woman stomping two feet in front, occasionally turning to the man and hissing something at him. The guy was keeping his face blank. Rick could relate to that. He kept his face blank now. A nice thing broke through too, almost made him smile. A happy kid saying, "Mom, what's the opposite of nobody being there?" Mom answering, "One person being there." "No," another of her kids said. "The opposite would be nobody being there. *Mo-o-om*, the opposite would be nobody being there."

Then he spotted his parents and grandparents waiting for him at the gate. His feeling of joy was accompanied by a feeling of isolation. He knew they wouldn't understand him anymore. He felt as if the world were divided between those who had been to Nam and those who hadn't.

"Rick!"

Rick rushed over. "Mom. Dad. Hey, Grandpa, Grandma." Everybody hugged him.

"I brought you extra clothes," said his mother. "I thought you might not have any."

The soldiers who weren't being met by anyone looked around tentatively. "Baby killer!" a woman called out. Somebody was talking to *Rick*. Several people glared his way.

"You talking to *me*?" he snapped back.

"Let's get you changed," his father said. "It's not worth fighting over. You'd have to fight half the country."

Rick changed in the bathroom. When he emerged, nobody glared at him anymore. A part of him wanted to put his uniform back on. He wasn't scared to fight half the country. But instead, he quietly followed his dad. When they got in the car, he immediately asked, "So, do you know if they heard anything about my dog?"

His father looked straight into his eyes. "Sorry, son" was all he said. And Rick could tell he really was.

And then he was home. Pancakes, lace on windows. He tried to feel happy to be here, but the thing that had been in his chest was in his stomach now. What used to seem like the real world now seemed like a fake. He wrote more letters but without the same fervor. He even wrote to the principal at his old high school. You never knew who might help.

He heard nothing for a few weeks. Many nights he sat alone on a lawn chair out back, staring at the streetlamps rising from the next street. His parents kept reminding him that he needed to start training to take over the store someday.

The family home had a great backyard. Trees everywhere. As a kid, he'd loved the sound of the branches tapping the windows. But lately he would lie lonely in bed, listening to the branches hit his window during an occasional breeze and feeling annoyed by the sound. So his math teacher had been wrong all along. This was what applying your-self all came down to: silence, then wind and the tapping of branches. Even he had to smile at that. Pretty poetic, if he did say so himself.

One night at dinner his dad said, "So, what about a job? You going to spend the rest of your life writing letters about a dead dog?"

Rick could have answered a lot of things, but he didn't answer at all. Then he said, "I talked to my buddy John about a job at his security firm." He paused. "I'm gonna get my own place."

His mother looked aghast, but he knew he

couldn't stay here. He'd been to Vietnam. He didn't belong in a house with lace curtains.

Over the past weeks Rick had imagined he'd heard the phone ring so many times that it took him a moment to realize that it really was ringing now. At first nobody moved. Then Rick pushed up off his chair and ran to the kitchen phone. "Hello?"

Thirty

Rick could hardly hear the voice on the other end of the line. "Who? What?" He could tell that the caller was shouting, but he still couldn't quite make out what he was saying. But it sounded like—could it be?—Cody. The static suddenly cleared.

". . . I said, it's Cody!"

"Cody! Are you back?"

"I'm DEROSing next week. Did you hear what I said?"

"You're DEROSing next week. Hey, congratulations."

"No, what I said before that. They found her. They found Cracker alive. She's shipping home!"

"What?!"

"They're shipping about two hundred of the

dogs back. Cracker's shipping into O'Hare. You got a pen? Let me give you the flight number. There's another guy waiting for the phone. Hello?"

Rick was already running to the drawer where they kept the pens, on the other side of the room. He shouted to his family staring at him from the table. "They got her! She's shipping back! Cracker's coming home!" Damn, what if Cody hung up? He ran back and snatched up the phone.

"Cody?"

"Yeah, you ready?"

"Yeah." His hands quivered as Cody spoke. *Damn, damn, damn!* The pen didn't work. He threw it down. "Hold on." He ran back to the drawer and pulled out a handful of pens. "Go."

Cody gave him the flight information. Rick's heart pounded as hard as it had when he'd been under contact. His handwriting looked like he had some kind of shaking disease. He asked Cody to repeat the information, just to make sure he had it down correctly.

As Cody told him the details again, Rick noticed something funny in Cody's voice. His own happiness faded slightly. "Did Bruno make it?"

"Nah," Cody said, so softly Rick almost didn't hear. "The dogs who weren't put to sleep were given to the South Vietnamese Army. Some other dogs got put down, but I begged for Bruno's life. Now I think she would have been better off put to sleep. The ARVN probably . . ." He didn't finish, but Rick knew what he was thinking: They probably ate or killed Bruno. Rick could hear the huge effort in Cody's voice as he struggled to say, "Nobody knows what happened to them after we gave them away." Another pause. "I played with him all day." He choked up. "We played on the obstacle course. Cracker was there. I didn't call you sooner because I didn't know if she was going to make it . . . so many of them went down."

"I'm sorry," said Rick. "I'm really sorry."

"Hey, I'm happy for you." But Rick got the feeling that Cody would never be the same kind of happy that he'd been a year ago.

"I gotta go," Cody said. "See you back in the world."

"Definitely," Rick said.

The phone clicked dead.

Rick took in a breath.

That night Rick listened to the scraping branches. They sounded different from yesterday. Less lonely. He sat up, looked at his clock. Ten thirty p.m. *So what?* He went through his drawer of letters, found one from Willie with his phone number in it. Rick's own parents had been in bed for half an hour.

He dialed a number, and a man answered, sounding annoyed. "Hello?"

Thirty-one

A WEEK LATER RICK WAS STANDING IN HIS uniform in the airport in Chicago, waiting for a crate to be unloaded in the baggage area. Who knew why it took a whole week to process Cracker? He was probably lucky it had taken such a short time, actually. They probably could have quarantined her for half a year if they'd wanted. But apparently, Twenty's uncle had a lot of pull.

For some reason, Rick felt he owed it to Cracker to wear his uniform. Probably a *dinky dau* idea, but so far there'd been just a few glares. A couple of other guys in uniform were also waiting for their baggage one carousel down. He nodded at them, and they nodded back.

A moment later he saw one of them in a scuffle

with a civilian. He limped over to help, but some other people had already broken up the fight.

As he returned to his carousel, he spotted a boy, a woman, and a man running toward two guys who were setting down a dog crate. He hurried toward them and heard the boy shouting with despair.

"No! Oh no!" the boy called out as he stared into the crate. Rick reached the crate and knelt down.

"Something's wrong with her!" cried the boy.

Rick peered inside: It was her! For a second his blood seemed to stop flowing. She lay on her side, not visibly breathing. But then he saw her ribs expand. She was just tranquilized, probably a little overtranquilized. He yanked open the gate.

Cracker's head hurt, and she felt sleepy. It seemed she'd been sleeping for a long, long time. She'd dreamed about the jungle, about Rick, about lizards, about rats. But now she smelled something . . . something important . . . very important. *Wiener!* She opened her eyes and staggered out of the cage, falling into Rick's arms.

She weakly pushed her head into his. Felt nice. Felt wonderful.

Twenty-Twenty, Camel, everybody had come through for Rick. Apparently, his father had even made some calls. Even that crazy fart U-Haul had made some calls—Rick had heard that from Twenty. As far as he knew, he was the only dog handler in the entire U.S. Army who had gotten his dog back. Fewer than two hundred dogs had escaped death, and all but Cracker were going to remain in the service until they died of old age.

His first words to Cracker were, "Want a wiener, nuthead?"

She wagged her tail, and he handed her a whole wiener at once. Gulp! One less wiener in the world!

Then Rick remembered the boy beside him. It had to be Willie.

He stood up and shook hands with Willie. "Thanks for coming."

"Thanks for calling me!"

Cracker wobbled confusedly for a moment as Willie knelt down to hold her. Wait a second . . . she belonged to Rick now. She wanted Rick.

"You think you can carry the crate to my car?" Rick asked. "I'll carry Cracker."

"Sure!"

Rick looked at Cracker. She'd lost a lot of weight, but she still had to weigh about ninety. Could he carry that much? He was pretty much rehabbed, but once in a while when he put too much weight on his leg, pain stabbed through it. He thought of Camel and told himself, *I* will *do it*. He would carry her, even with his weak leg. He took in a breath, lifted Cracker, and winced as the weight fell on his bad leg. "Ahhh," he moaned.

"You want me to help?" Willie asked.

"No, I'm cool."

As he walked, he tried—unsuccessfully, he knew—to keep from limping, to keep up that tough veneer. But as he carried her, he knew he didn't look tough, and he knew people were staring, and he knew he didn't give a can of beans what they thought. Man, she was still heavy.

Willie walked alongside him, his dad helping him tote the dog crate. "Will you let me come visit you sometimes?" the boy asked.

"Sure."

"Was she the best dog in Vietnam? She was, wasn't she?"

"Yup."

"Was she brave? She was, wasn't she?"

"Yup."

"Your letter said she saved a lot of lives?"

"Yup." Rick paused, looked right at Willie. "She saved mine, too."

Willie's eyes grew wide. "For real?"

Rick grinned. "Yup."

"Rick?" Willie's face was serious.

"Yeah?"

"I understand."

"Understand what?" They both stopped.

"How she's your dog now. I understand. But thank you for letting me see her."

Rick didn't know what to say to that. Then he said, "You did good. Don't ever forget that."

In the parking lot Willie and his father set down the crate and Rick set down Cracker.

Willie's parents shook hands with Rick. "Thank you for calling us. It meant so much to Willie," said Willie's mother. "We thought he'd get over it, but he didn't, and we—well, we just want to thank you for calling us. Willie's been so emotional throughout all this."

"Mom, you're acting like I'm a baby," Willie said.

"I'm just trying to explain."

Willie looked at Rick and rolled his eyes.

Rick patted Willie's shoulder and said, "Thanks for helping with the crate. I gotta get her home now, but we'll be seeing each other. You come up and visit."

"I sure will!"

They looked at each other. Rick saw something in the boy's eyes. He studied Willie a moment before realizing the kid wanted to cry. He reached into his pocket. "Hey, look, want my dogtags?"

"Sure!" Willie eagerly took the tags. Then he knelt down before Cracker and hugged her close, the way he had the last time he'd seen her. And he felt the hug way down inside himself. He whispered in her ear, "You'll always be my dog. I made you the best dog in Vietnam."

Cracker got up and shook herself off. Her head was clearing. Instead of feeling happy, she felt sad. She thought that now she was going back to Willie.

She put her tail between her legs. Rick laughed. "Guess she's being kind of shy."

Then, instead of crying, Willie stood up and shook Rick's hand like a man would. And Rick said the same thing that Willie had just whispered: "You made her the best dog in Vietnam."

Despite Willie's promise to himself that he wasn't going to cry, a few teardrops trickled down his cheeks as he watched Rick throw the crate into his backseat. Then the Stetson family slowly walked off, waving back all the while.

Cracker felt relief as Rick signaled to her to hop into the front of his car. She was still his dog after all.

Then Rick climbed into his old, beat-up Chevy

Malibu—all he could afford at the moment. He turned the ignition, heard it click, and sighed. He took out the hammer he kept in the glove compartment and got out of the car. He popped the hood, gave the solenoid a couple of taps, and got back in. The car started.

"Don't worry, we'll get a better car soon," he told Cracker.

He'd already found his own apartment, and his friend had helped him get that job at a security firm. It wasn't going to be a perfect life for a big dog, but it was the best he could do for now. He'd take Cracker out for walks, and they could go camping on the weekends. There was room for growth at the firm, especially since the boss was thinking about opening a guard dog department. Or maybe Rick would eventually take up his uncle's offer and move to Los Angeles to learn carpentering.

Cracker climbed into his lap as he backed up. He was the luckiest handler in America. Rick peered around Cracker to drive. "Down, girl," he said, and she lay on his thighs.

Rick drove down the expressway in Chicago. Some war protestors were holding up signs along the way. But Rick didn't resent it, didn't even care anymore. He'd killed men, seen men and dogs die, seen courage, and felt it too. He'd smelled the metallic blood-scent in the air, and he had come back whole.

Had he survived all that to be angry?

Cracker lay with satisfaction in his lap. She smelled another wiener in his pocket, but she didn't paw him yet. She knew he would give it to her soon. She knew somehow that there was plenty of time for more wieners. Plenty of time!

Author's Note

DOGS HAVE SERVED THE UNITED STATES IN A NUMBER OF conflicts, including World War II, the Korean War, the Vietnam War, the Gulf War, and the Iraq War.

During the Vietnam War, dogs were considered military equipment; at the war's end they were considered *surplus* military equipment. Although precise records were not kept, most historians agree that at least 4,000 dogs served during the war, and are credited with saving some 10,000 human lives. About 1,000 dogs died in country from combat, jungle diseases, or other reasons. At war's end, only approximately 200 dogs were reassigned to other U.S. military bases. The remaining dogs were either euthanized or given to the South Vietnamese Army. The fate of those dogs remains unknown.

After the Vietnam War, military policy was changed to allow war dogs to come home. Today the policy is known as No Military Working Dog Left Behind. Further information can be obtained at the Vietnam Dog Handlers Association's website: www.vdhaonline.org.

To meet the demands of my story, I have made some changes from historical fact. There was no 67th IPSD. Most notable is that I have changed the timeline so a few things that really happened early in the war—such as an entire platoon shipping out battle ready—happen later in the war in my book. Though this book is based on fact, it is a work of fiction, and should be viewed as such.

Acknowledgments

I'D LIKE TO THANK THE FOLLOWING VIETNAM DOG handlers who submitted to interviews for this book: Rick Claggett, Bob Himrod, Mike Lister, Bud Rhea, and Ollie Whetstone. Most of them in their generosity allowed me to interview them more than once. Thanks as well to the late Robert Russell, who served as a veterinary technician. In particular, I'd like to thank Rick, who I badgered relentlessly both on the phone and via e-mail and who was absolutely magnanimous.

I'd also like to thank those dog handlers who read the manuscript for errors: Rick Claggett, Bob Himrod, Mike Lister, and J. Thomas Sykes. Tom also answered many questions at length via e-mail. Thanks also to writer Mike Lemish for reading the manuscript and providing comments.

I'm greatly appreciative of Special Forces Soldier Eulis Presley, who was generous, patient, and brimming with information and insight during our multiple interviews, some of which lasted hours. Special Forces Soldier John Blackadar as well provided great insights during our interview. I'd also like to express my appreciation to them both for taking the time to read the Special Forces section, in Eulis's case twice.

Patricia L. Walsh, who served as a nurse in country, allowed me to interview her repeatedly. She also read the section that takes place in the hospital twice, as well as other sections for context. I was struck by the bigness of her heart during our discussions.

Dr. Clarence Sasaki, who served in a hospital in Vietnam during the war, took time out from his busy schedule for an interview. Dr. Sasaki is the Charles W. Ohse Professor of Surgery and the Chief of Otolaryngology–Head and Neck Surgery at the Yale School of Medicine.

And thanks to Betty Rowe for her interview about giving up her dog to serve in Vietnam.

Thanks also to Dan Schilling for our conversation about his return from Vietnam.

Finally, *cám ón* to the eagle eyes of Jeannie Ng and Cindy Nixon, who have saved me from disgrace once again. And thanks to Amy Lerner for helping me finish the manuscript, and my niece, Caroline, for her enthusiastic input.

War Dogs With Their Handlers in the Vietnam Era

Dog Handler Mike Lister and Dutchy of the 25th IPSD on obstacle course in Tay Ninh, 1969. The 25th IPSD was assigned to the 1st Air Cavalry Division. (Photo by Peter Nelson)

Dog handler Ollie Whetstone (44th IPSD) writing a letter home as his dog, Eric (36X3), watches after the famous Battle of LZ Gold in March 1967. (Photo courtesy of Ollie Whetstone)

Dogs in training in An Khe, Vietnam. (Photo by Robert Russell)

Sergeant Tom Sykes and his partner, Royal, of the army's 48th IPSD, 196th Light Infantry Brigade, Americal Division. Photo taken in 1968 while at the unit's base camp located on Landing Zone Baldy. (Photo by Cecil Pendleton)

Big Boy and his handler, Rick Claggett, in front of the sign for their unit. Photo taken in Vietnam in 1971. (Photo courtesy of Rick Claggett)

PRAISE FOR CYNTHIA KADOHATA:

"Kadohata stays true to the child's viewpoint in plain, beautiful prose that can barely contain the passionate feelings." —*Booklist*

"[A] luminous new voice in fiction . . ." —*New York Times*

"Masterful in her evocation of physical, spiritual, and cultural displacement." —*Los Angeles Times*

Cracker is one of the United States Army's most valuable weapons.

She's a German shepherd trained to sniff out bombs, traps, and enemy soldiers. The safety of everyone around her depends on her keen sense of smell and intelligence.

Soldier Rick Hanski is headed to war. He wants to show the world, especially his father and his sergeant, that he has what it takes to be a great soldier. But sometimes Rick wonders if he really is capable of facing the challenges of battle.

When Cracker is paired with Rick, it isn't easy for either of them. They need to be friends before they can be a team, and they must be a team if they want to get home alive.

Join a dog and his soldier as they develop a deep friendship in this unforgettable book from Newbery Medal–winning author Cynthia Kadohata.

This book is only available in the school book club and school book fair market.

ALADDIN PAPERBACKS
Simon & Schuster, New York
Cover designed by Sammy Yuen
Cover illustration © 2007 by Shane Rebenschied
Ages 10 up
SimonSaysKids.com
0808

US $7.99 / $9.50 CAN
ISBN-13: 978-1-4169-7522-9
ISBN-10: 1-4169-7522-5
BC
50799
EAN
9 781416 975229